THE MERCHANT'S DREAM

Zak Attioui

Published by Hidden Archive Press.
First published in 2019.
Hidden Archive Press edition published in 2026.

ISBN: 979-8-9963529-0-6

Printed in the United States of America

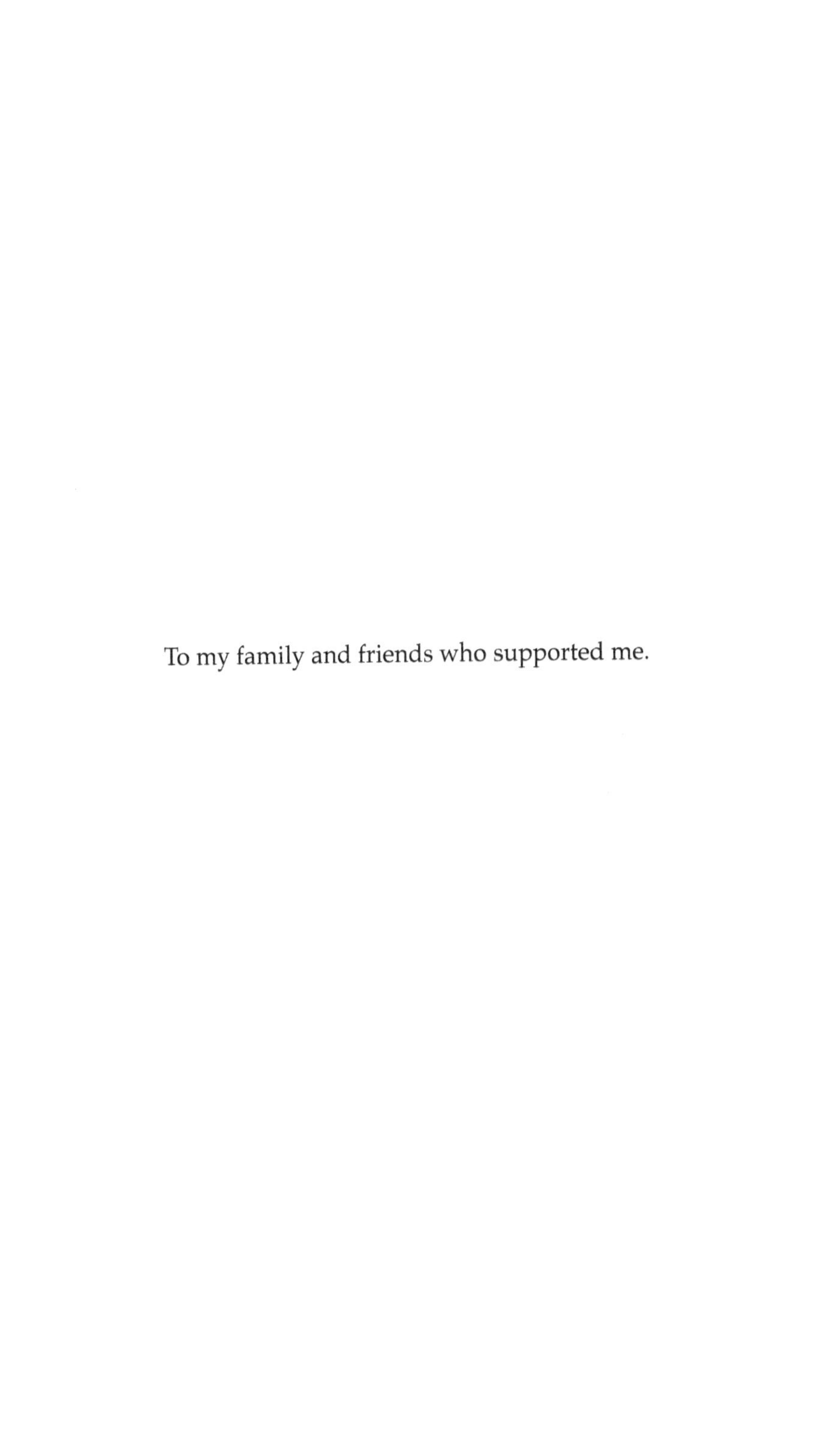

To my family and friends who supported me.

1

My parents appeared in my dreams, the fourth time in three nights.

I sat near the window, listening to the howling wind. My adoptive father told me dreams have no weight. He shared few details about my parents. And I could faintly remember their faces. Or at least, I thought those faces were theirs. The wind rattled the window frame. I pressed my forehead against the glass and watched the empty street until the feeling passed. Then I went to get ready for the market. Saturdays were the busiest.

The apartment was small enough that I knew every sound it made. I walked through the hall, listening for movement ahead. Bouchra's snoring through the bedroom door. The way the floorboards near the bathroom creaked differently depending on who was walking on them. And then there was the drip from the kitchen tap. Each drop brought the dream back. The rush of water. My parents are standing in front of it. I stood there a moment longer than I needed to. Then I opened the tap and washed my face. Ahmed was clearing his throat near the bathroom as I returned to the living room.

I stood when Ahmed entered the living room. "Salam, Ahmed," I said, eyeing his left hip. It still pained him, and he would not admit the fact. He nodded in response. Ahmed grunted as he took his seat; I followed in pursuit without a sound. He leaned over the table and brought the oil lamp closer. Though we had electricity, he chose oil lamps as the home's primary light source.

It would be easier to use the electricity, I thought, watching him struggle with the thumbwheel. I dared not voice my thoughts. "Would you like me to help?" I asked. He would say no. I knew his response, but I still offered.

We sat in silence for a few minutes, the dream of my parents sitting heavily in my mind. I wanted to ask him about them. Whether he still had contact with them. I could not gather enough courage. I already knew how it would end. A shrug. A subject changed. The question dissolved before it reached my lips. The kitchen tap dripped into the silence. And then Bouchra opened the creaking bedroom door. Despite his old age, Ahmed heard even the slightest sound.

"Old lady, where is the breakfast?" Ahmed waved a hand in the hallway's direction. "It is Saturday, and you know—"

"Old man, could you not have at least put water in the kettle?" She retorted.

I watched Ahmed's dried lips. For a fraction of a second, the ends curled. Despite his grouchy attitude with almost everyone, he had a soft spot for Bouchra.

We ate in silence, mostly. Mint tea, olive oil, bread. Bouchra set a plate of scrambled eggs in front of me without a word.

"Thank you, Bouchra," I said. She smiled and took her seat beside Ahmed.

"Push over." She nudged him. "You want the entire spot for yourself?"

"No, old lady, I will share." He grunted and shifted toward me. "The red rug. How long until it's complete?"

"Not for another three days." Bouchra broke off a piece of bread. "What do you think of it?"

"One of your better rugs."

She smiled again. I watched them and thought about my

parents. Whether they sat like this in the mornings. Whether they argued about small things and meant none of it. I wanted a moment to isolate Bouchra and ask her about them. Though she never had much to say, she was more open to those conversations. Ahmed had told her something. I was certain of it.

I finished my eggs and said nothing.

I waited at the door, wearing a long sleeve shirt and linen pants. Ahmed left the bedroom with a brown blazer and dress pants. He only wore blazers, one of two colors, brown or black. They suited him well; his short, square body matched well with the blazer. He led the way out the door, in his typical slow walk. I followed one step behind.

As we walked to the shop, I wondered how much money I'd make from working. Ahmed gave me the money he thought I deserved after each workday, and it all depended on how many customers bought our rugs. It was always a reasonable amount.

We were usually one of the first shops to open. Many similar rug shops were nearby.

The dream preoccupied my thoughts as we approached the shop. Four times in three nights. I rarely thought much of my dreams. I couldn't get this one off my mind. It was so vivid not to be true.

Ahmed took his usual seat in the back of the shop once we arrived. A long table stretched across the shop, like a counter, with a flap to allow us to move around to the other side. Ahmed dealt with counting the money, while I started the conversation with the customers. He would provide the customers with a more detailed response if I couldn't. Sometimes, when Ahmed didn't require my help, I assisted other shops. The only ones I stayed away from were other rug shops. Ahmed's shop was my priority, and I didn't want to lose any of our customers.

A familiar customer walked in first. I noticed him as he had come a few days ago. But what caught my attention most was the rug he was holding. It was not a good sign that a customer returned with a rug bought days ago. Ahmed's attitude in these situations was very strict. I sprang to my feet and tried to keep the man hidden from Ahmed's line of sight.

"Salam," I said to the man, eyeing him and the rug. I wore a smile, hoping it would lighten his dark face. He ignored my peace greeting and walked around me to the shop's entrance.

The man entered the shop with a swear word. I hesitated, suddenly overtaken by the shivering in my legs. I hated arguments and fights. Ahmed started yelling, and his words were not good either. He remained behind the counter while the tall man showed the rug and explained the problem.

"The rug ripped in less than a month. Is this what you do, sell cheap rugs? I want my money back, and you can take the rug back."

Ahmed laughed at the man's face. He almost always had a straight face. For arguments, he made a joke of the people he argued with. "You want all your money back and for me to hand you a ripped rug? Let me ask you—"

"The quality is not—"

"*Let* me ask you, young man." Ahmed sharpened his voice. He was no longer laughing or smiling, back to his serious face. "When I sold you the rug, did it have those rips? No. When I sold you the rug, did you pay me the full amount of three hundred dirhams? Yes. Now you want me to buy that ripped rug from you and pay you back?" Ahmed's serious expression broke into hysterical laughter. He started tapping the glass counter with his palm.

The man swore some more, pacing around the shop, looking as if he wanted to break things. I held the fear inside me and looked out of the shop. A few people, in the far distance, were looking over at our shop. It had still been early morning; our neighboring shops hadn't opened yet. My legs still shook with fear of the man's shouting and swearing. I turned to them. The man held the rug with the rip visible. He would not budge, and

Ahmed stood behind the counter, both forearms resting on the glass counter, watching the man with a serious expression. I looked closely at the rip.

It had not been a terrible rip, and it had been one of Bouchra's handmade living room rugs. If I remembered correctly, it had been a week's worth of work, not much compared to the more complex and larger ones. The larger ones were well over a thousand dirhams, some even surpassing the two-thousand mark. With this being three hundred dirhams, I had an idea.

"We will give you a discount," I told the man. He quickly looked me over and puffed out a breath. As a young kid, I often got it from older customers. They never took me seriously as a valid merchant in the market. I entered behind the counter and mouthed something in Ahmed's ear. "I thought maybe we'd give him a refund, but keep a fourth to ourselves as compensation. I do not think it's a bad fix; Bouchra can fix it in a day at most. We keep a fourth and the rug. Bouchra fixes the rug and we sell it at full price. What do you think?"

Ahmed turned to the man. "Let me see the rug."

The man tossed the rug onto the glass countertop. Ahmed gave him a heavy glance and then inspected the rug. He made a few grunts and sighs. "People cannot take care of the things they buy and then come crying for a refund." He placed both hands on the rug and then looked at the man. The man opened his mouth, from the expression on his face, to start arguing, but Ahmed cut him off. "I will offer you this. I do not do this with damaged rugs. I will take the rug back and keep a fourth of your payment."

"Is this what you do? "Sell cheap rugs, and then, when they return with them, keep an amount to yourself?"

"No, I am doing you a favor." Ahmed said, pushing the rug closer to the man's side of the counter. "If you don't accept, take your rug and leave my shop."

The man stood silently to himself for a moment. And then he said, "I want four-fifths."

"No," Ahmed said instantly.

A fifth of the amount, and the rug was worth it. I had a strong feeling Ahmed knew of this after assessing the rug. An easy fix and an easy too, but he decided to play hard. It had been a skill Ahmed, and all the experienced merchants, possessed. Bargaining.

"It's ripped. I paid three hundred for the rug. I should get a full refund. If you're going to cheat me for a refund, then you have to give me two hundred and forty dirhams."

"I do not have to refund you, young man." Ahmed went to the safe on the other side of the counter. "Go ask any merchant, wherever you go in Morocco, and they will tell you the same thing. You buy something, you can exchange it after a few days. If the item is damaged, go ask any merchant; they will not give you a refund. What I did now is doing you a favor." He licked his thumb and started counting the money, placing the notes on the counter. "I will give you two hundred and forty, and you have this young man to thank. If it were me and you, I would have told you to leave my shop and you would not get a single dirham from me."

You have the young man to thank, I reiterated Ahmed's words with a smile. Compliments from him were rare, especially in front of others. I always believed that he appreciated my assistance, it was just hard for him to speak of it.

The man grabbed the money and left the shop. He was muttering something under his breath, but I could not pick up the exact words.

"We did well. Even at that price, we can still fix this and sell it for the same price."

Ahmed placed a hand on my unruly hair. "Thanks to your young mind."

Bouchra opened the door. "Did the old man forget something?"

I gave her my best smile. "No, he no longer has pills at the shop. Told me to return and ask you for more."

She nodded to herself. "I will grab them for you."

I followed, my mind working for ideas on how I could bring the dream into the discussion. She went into the bedroom, and I stood near the door. There really was no way for me to plan my discussion with her. Not because she was unexpected, but because my mind worked better when I went with the flow.

"I had multiple dreams about my parents. Four in three nights."

The room had two oil lamps burning on opposite sides. She paused at my statements, and then continued onward to the opposite end of the room as I continued.

"When we last talked about them, I really wanted to see if you knew anything about them. Maybe where they are or... anything."

She turned. "Ahmed would know more—"

I nodded to her statement until she paused. "I know, Bouchra, but I always try to talk to him about it, and he just tells me it doesn't matter or figures a way to... It's the same dream; four times in three nights." I lowered my head. I could not speak ill of Ahmed. I could not speak ill of anyone. But I also wanted her to tell me something, anything, about my parents.

She narrowed her eyes for a moment and then searched the drawer. "Explain the dream."

My body lit up at those words. She was never curious enough to ask for more details. It was for that reason that our conversation then had more weight than our previous conversations about the dreams. So, I told her. All the details, or at least, as much as I could remember. I knew there were parts of the dream that I could not remember.

"My parents were both there, kneeling before me with their hands tied. A rush of water sounded behind them; it sounded like a waterfall, but I could not say if it was or not clearly. A blur was behind them, too. Their eyes were looking up at me, sorrowful eyes. Maybe even begging me for something."

By then she had found the pills and turned and started to

walk in my direction. Bouchra, unlike Ahmed, wore emotions on her face. She looked deeply worried; she tucked both hands inside her bathrobe pockets as if to hide her shaky hands. But I knew too well about her actions, hers and Ahmed's. It was the perfect time to get information from her; she was vulnerable. I had to evoke her emotions.

"I am worried, Bouchra. I know you said that Ahmed knows about them. But you must know something, too. Please. I will not leave and—"

She shook her head. "It's not about leaving, my dear boy. But the dream you had, it is awfully troubling. Four times in three nights, you said. Very troubling." She gave me the box of pills— her hand was shaking—and then grabbed my elbow, taking me out into the hall.

My heart beat faster. What did she mean by the dream being troubling?

"When I was a young girl, a family friend had a bad dream, repeatedly. A nightmare, she told her parents. They happened multiple times, sometimes within the same night. The dream aspect seems similar to what you explained, but yours doesn't sound like a nightmare. Her parents took her to a physician and then to an imam. The dream became worse and worse; the dream also changed slightly. She never shared the dream details with anyone until the day before she ran away. In the dream, her older brother starved and became thin after each dream. As for her older sister, she went crazy after sometime. Her brother died months later from malnutrition. Even when he ate, it was as if he had eaten nothing. My family told me that the girl ran away following her brother's death. How long have you had this dream?"

"Since last week," I said absently.

"You will be fine," she said, kissing my head. "From you told me, it's not a nightmare like hers, and I am sure your parents are doing fine."

I stared blankly for some time. The image of my parents'

sorrowful eyes and tied hands. I asked myself, what if my parents were in trouble. It no longer was a matter of wanting to learn about my parents, but now it became a matter of saving them, somehow. I could not allow my dream, like the girl's, to happen to them.

"You should go," Bouchra said, walking me to the door. "Ahmed might not always tell you, but he really appreciates your help at the market. He always tells me."

I looked at her with a forced smile. Though the words would have brought me true happiness, at that moment, they did the opposite.

She stuck a stick in a spinning wheel; I thought of the saying. I walked to the rug shop with heavy legs; I had to choose between staying with Ahmed and Bouchra or finding my parents. And from the girl's dream, I had little time.

2

For the next two days, I had the dream once a night. On the third morning, on a Tuesday morning, the location of the dream came into mind. It was as if the location dropped onto my mind. Or at least the general location. I pushed the bedsheet, and scrambled for a piece of paper and pencil. I wrote down as much details as I could, knowing that I typically forgot most of the dream minutes after I woke up.

I started with the new details. Crowds behind my parents. Hazy skies, though it looked like a clear sky. And the large dunes from the west. The sun rose from behind the dunes. I thought for a moment, bitting on the end of the pencil. Or was it a sunset that came from behind the dunes. I wrote the detail and allow the contemplation come later. Once the new details were on the paper, I went ahead and wrote the core details, ones that I had already dreamt about many times over. My parents with their hands tied in of front of themselves, on their knees.

Sitting crosslegged, I stared at the notes with mixed feelings. I felt as though I should be happy, knowing that I had a general direction of where my parents were but I could not get through the fact that to find my parents, I had to first break through a wall.

The bedroom door creaked open from across the hall. Ahmed's grunting followed. No matter what, I had to get his approval.

My parents were somewhere near the desert, that, I could conclude from that morning's dream. A critical detail, one that I could not confirm if it had meaning or not without Ahmed or Bouchra telling me about their location, or where they adopted me. And from the sun, the scene could have been from either end, from Morocco's side of the Sahara Desert or Egypt's side. I hoped it was Morocco's side.

During breakfast, I itched to share with Bouchra and Ahmed the new addition. The words waited at my lips. I looked in their direction a couple times. Ahmed continued pressing against his left hip. He grunted and moaned to himself. I turned to my breakfast—homemade bread with a hardboiled egg and some cheese. My longing to find out more burned inside, I could feel it within my heart. That sensation paved the path for the question. Before I knew it, I dropped the question.

"Were my parents Moroccan? I had the dream about them again last night."

I flushed red at my question. I had the urge to leave the room, to apologize and leave. But I could not. The part of me who wanted answers kept the scared me quiet. Despite the urge to leave the room, hide somewhere, I continued eating without daring to look at Ahmed or Bouchra. From the corner of my eyes, I noticed his heavy gaze on me. It definitely had not been the right time to ask the question, not when he had other problems like the aching hip. Even I had not been myself. But seeing the dream multiple times, of a couple I knew almost certainly were my parents, made me anxious and irritable.

"I have told you multiple times, you are living with us now. You are our son, not by last name, but I treat you as my own. Whatever dreams you have do not matter, of whoever it may be." Ahmed said with calculated words.

For a moment, I said nothing and considered his words. He was right. But me asking also did not negate my curiosity of knowing about my real parents. The fact he did not want to tell me, only told me that he had something to hide. I had always had this suspicion. I rose my cup of tea and drank, taking a quick glance at Bouchra. Her attention fell on Ahmed, watching him and possibly had something in her mind. She knew better than to speak, especially against his words.

"Does it repeat?" Bouchra asked. "Is it the same exact one or an alternation?"

"Same one," I told her, finally raising my gaze in their direction. "It happened multiple times—"

"Stop!" Ahmed shouted. He glared at me; I lowered my head to the table. My legs trembled in fear. "I told you, stop with the questions and the dream. It means nothing! And even if it meant something, your parents left you to others to raise. We have accepted to raise you, cared for you, provided for you, and I have worked hard so that you can have the shop after I leave this world, all this, and you still care about some dream or who your parents are?" Ahmed grunted and placed the empty glass cup on the table hard. "I say, you are not showing me that you appreciate our care."

"I do, Ahmed. I really do!" I could not say where I found the strength to speak those words. In that moment, I felt a level of fear and shame that I had never felt before. I felt like an idiot to question him. I felt pulled by both arms—to obey Ahmed and to find my parents.

"No you don't," he told me and then turned to Bouchra "More tea. If you did, you will listen to what I have to say and will not ask these questions again. This is your life. Merchant under me, and then, when you get married or I die, you can have my shop. Is that not good enough for you?"

I had never felt worse. All these years, Ahmed never mention about giving me his shop when I got married or when he passed away. I suspected it, and it made sense as he and Bouchra had no children. But that piece of detail made me feel like I had been in the wrong, that I should completely forget about the dream, act like it had been nothing—even if it meant my parents were in danger—and appreciate the good Ahmed provided me. He taught me the art of selling and Bouchra educated me so that I did not have to attend school.

"I am sorry," I said, promising myself that I would never bring the question to light.

Despite the warm Tuesday, with clear skies and warm breeze, the market had a sense of darkness that I rarely noticed. Ahmed and I shared very few words that morning. I sold a few small rugs. And we also had a few foreign visitors who were white. I spoke with them in broken English. Whenever the foreigners came around, I tried to learn a few words—whether that was in English or French or even German. I had learned a few words from them. They were the highlight of the morning.

I looked over to Ahmed after they left, trying to gage his feelings. It had been difficult to figure out as he always had a serious resting face. I thought of something to say, something that would make him happy. Thankfully, I knew him well in that regard. Sitting next to the entrance and him sitting inside the shop, I turned my body so that it faced him.

"Times have changed Ahmed," I said wearing a smile. "We have seen more foreigners this year than the previous year." All I managed to get from him was a grunt. "Has it always been like this, like when you were a little kid?"

Ahmed looked in my direction, his gaze held my eyes for a long moment. I could read his eyes, it seemed like he knew my goals for the question. If there was anything that he loved talking about, it had been about old times. He loved reminiscing about his childhood and when he was my age. We had our share of conversation, and the times I remember him genuinely happen, was when we spoke of those times.

"We grow old, and a new generation follows," he said. "The next generation will have those people among us more than the previous generations."

Ahmed raised a finger and pointed outside. I briefly followed the direction of his finger. A couple of white people walked side by side. When I looked back, he had looked away and picked up a needle and tried sticking some yarn inside the small hole. I stood to help him, but he waved me off.

"Sit back down," he told me. "I will handle it."

From then, we sat in silence and only spoke briefly if a customer came into our shop. By midday, I left Ahmed alone at the shop and went for a walk to clear my head. I knew the person I needed at the moment; the person who even if everything went wrong in his life, would still have a positive outlook.

Mohamed sold chicken and turkey eggs. It had been his trade, buying and reselling eggs. He traveled a distance from his farm, everyday to sell eggs. Early in the morning, he settled the eggs in between two shops and waited for customers to arrive. He would stay until he sold all the eggs or when sunset approached the horizon.

"Salam, Mohamed," I said, with a polite tone but loud enough for him to hear. I noticed that this past year, he started to have difficulty in hearing. "Do you have eggs for me?"

He squinted his eyes, and then greeted me with a smile. "Darius. Waalaikumsalam. Of course. You can have them all." He sat on the sidewalk with a cushion for more comfort. He tried pulling it out, as if it to handle it to me.

I smiled at his kind-hearted gesture. "No, please. Keep it. I will sit on the edge of the sidewalk." I sat close to him. Despite him not making much money, he smelled of oud—mostly likely bought a small bought from near the mosque.

"How are you doing? I haven't seen you in a long time." He wore a wide smile that made the edges of his eyes wrinkle. His green eyes had a smile of their own.

"Great to hear you're doing well. I'm sorry I haven't been around; I've been so busy lately and have had much on my mind. I don't know how I should go about it so I came to ask for your advice."

"What is it, young man? I will try to help you as much as I can," he replied, pushing his chest out to straighten his back.

"I've had this same dream for the past few days, and I don't know what to do about it."

"What is the dream about, if you don't mind?" he asked politely. He watched me carefully. I stared at the eggs in front of him, considering of how I could relay the dream and what happened between Ahmed and I.

"I had this dream about my parents, and I'm not exactly sure if it's true or not. I know for sure it was my parents," I began, and broke down the details. I included some information about Ahmed and Bouchra but held off about their hesitation of about my parents.

When I finished, he sat there for a moment, in silence. I waited for him to speak but then a woman came by.

She turned his attention to him. "How much are the eggs?"

"Whatever you think is a good price. How many would you like?" Mohamed said, giving her a plastic bowl to collect her eggs.

I looked at Mohamed with wide eyes; my ears in disbelief of what he had told her. A merchant always gave the initial price. The customer always bargained for a lower price, merchants expected this. But never in my life had I heard a merchant look for the price.

The lady wore a jilabiya—a long dress that covered her entire body from neck to her ankles. She wore a headscarf, an old fashioned scarf. From the initial look of her, she looked about a few years younger than Bouchra.

"I asked another person at the other side street and told me twenty-six rial. I told him twenty-four and he said no. I will take ten for twenty-six rial, is that fine?"

"Yes, that it good price." Mohamed placed the plastic bowl in front of her. While she selected ten eggs, he took out a plastic bag from his jacket's pocket and transferred the eggs into the bag. He tied the bag, careful so that the eggs would not break. She pulled out thirty dirhams. They exchanged items. On the opposite jacket pocket, he took out a stack of coins and counted four dirhams and gave them to her.

"Why did you ask her for the price?" I asked when she left.

"Sometimes I only take what the people want to give me. Of course I know the price, most people will give a reasonable amount. Each egg will be about one dirham, give or take a couple rials. I also do this on certain days of the week, like Tuesdays, the day I was born. But for the organic eggs, I always have a price."

When he explained it like that, it became less shocking. It made sense, the price of eggs were already low. Unlike high priced items, eggs used rial in addition to dirhams. Customers had little room to bargain for a significant lower price—except if they bought many eggs which in that case, it benefited the merchant as well.

"Going back to our conversation, I would say to go. Find out for yourself if your dream is true or not," he told me gently. "You are still young, you gave no responsibilities. Why should you stay here when you desire to search for your parents."

I smiled—the first time someone told me what I wanted to hear. It sounded so good to my ears that I subconsciously followed up with a question, desiring to hear the words again. "Really, you think so?"

"Yes. You had the same dream many times, correct?"

"Yes, I did."

"Then you must go to confirm for yourself. It's not a matter of if you can or can't," Mohamed reassured me. His attention turned to the eggs. There were ten empty spots from the ten eggs the woman bought. From the other end, he had a large box of eggs. He pulled one after another and filled those ten empty spots.

"You're right. I need to figure out if it is true or not. Otherwise, I will live the rest of my life regretting for not trying."

"Exactly, young man. If you don't find them, you'll always be welcome here. I'll still be here, and Ahmed will be here too, unless our bodies give up," he said with a smile at the end.

I drifted into my own thoughts. Hearing Mohamed's words rose new thoughts. If I did not purse my the dream, or at least search for my parents, I would definitely regret it as I grow older. Regret and I are acquainted. I hold many memories of regretting not accepting a buyer's bargain offer for a rug. I also somewhat regret not asking Ahmed and Bouchra about continuing my education. Though I learned many skills as merchant, I could not but feel a sense of loneliness from not having friends my age. No matter what I wanted to choose—search for my parents or stay— I had one obstacle in my way.

"But what about Ahmed? He doesn't want me to go, and I don't want to leave him alone at the shop," I said.

"Ahmed had the rug shop before you came around. He can manage without you," he said. "Yes, he is getting old like myself, but we can still come out here and work. In my opinion, young man, it is in our best interest to continue moving everyday. If we are to stop working, or just sit down all day at our homes, we will die quicker. And I will say one more thing. If he cannot manage without you, he can always get a young man who wants to learn the trade to work for him while you're away. You will come back, won't you?"

"Of course," I said with a smile.

Mohamed ran a hand over my head. "You are becoming a man. In a few years, you might want to get married and start a family of your own. At that point, you have full control over your life. Right now, you should practice and see how life is without Ahmed around or someone close to you. Because when you have a family, others will look at you for answers. You have already taken a good step forward—asking people older than you for advice. I say do what *you* think is best for you."

"Uncle Mohamed," I said honoring him with uncle status, "you are the wisest person I know. Thank you so much for telling me this. Like you said, even if something goes wrong, it will be a learning experience. Better to learn now when I have no dependents than later, when I am responsible for others. Right now, I just need a way to convince Ahmed about all this."

Mohamed remained silent with a melancholy expression. I hoped he would say more, that he would talk to Ahmed or share something that would convince Ahmed that I had to leave. None of those happened which dimmed my excitement. I felt confident in leaving, but still, I had Ahmed in my way. And I did not want to escape at night. I wanted Ahmed and Bouchra's blessing.

"I have to go back," I said, getting on my feet.

"Well come back to say goodbye if you decide to leave," Mohamed said with a wide smile. We shook hands and I walked back to the rug shop, thinking of how I could convince Ahmed.

"Can I stay in the market for a few more minutes," I asked, putting the chair back inside. We had just prayed Asr at the small market mosque and Ahmed wanted to close early today. On the days he closed early, I typically walked around the market and either helped other merchants in change to learn their art of selling or I spoke with the merchants I knew, like Mohamed.

Ahmed nodded as a reply. So when we brought down the garage door, and he locked it for the night, we walked in separate paths. I went deeper into the market. Most markets, such as ours, had shops and stands bunched together. We were in the rug section; all shops in the market that sold rugs were around ours. I left this area and entered the fish section. The fish merchants wore large aprons and many of them were preparing to leave. Their stalls mostly empty, with a few leftover types of fishes.

The ones who had not sold everything, or still had more fish became more desperate to sell their fish before sunset. They yelled lower prices, seeking to attract more customers. I stepped away from one of the fish merchants. He threw water in front of his stall, and then used a special mop to bring the water down to the gutter that ran down the alley of stalls and shops.

I turned the corner and entered into the spices section. Those merchants had shops of their own, like ours, and were not as desperate to sell as the fish merchants. Most of them sat behind their crates of spices and either watched television, read books, or talked with their neighbors. I knew a few spice merchants. But at the time, they were not there. A stick ran across the small entrance through the boxes of spices; this told the customers that the merchant wasn't at their shop.

Around another corner, the spice scent became into a scent of chicken. Each shop had an enclosed area where chickens moved about. I looked into one of the shops. A man pulled a chicken from a large pot of boiling water and then dropped it on the cutting board. The boiling water made the feathers easier to remove. I continued onward; leaving the few dozen chicken merchants.

I headed for the center, where there was produce. But as I reached the end of the chicken merchants, I spotted someone that made me stop. Ahmed stood with Mohamed; I could see partially their backs and their sides. Seeing them together sparked my interest. Ahmed held a bag of bananas and apples. I could not hear their words, they were at least ten meters ahead. It seemed that Mohamed did most of the talking while Ahmed listened. And then, after about a minute or two, they talked in equal amounts.

Occasionally, Ahmed turned his head slightly toward my way, so I managed to capture a glimpse of his face. I leaned more optimistic and Ahmed had a neutral expression. Which in his standards was like a positive expression. And with Mohamed there, I could only hope that their conversation made mention of me. I smiled with excitement.

What if Mohamed managed to convince Ahmed that I could leave?

I stood there for a couple more minutes, watching their

interaction with full attention. But with a sudden surprise, Ahmed turned around to my direction. I had as quick of a reaction. The moment he turned, the moment I did so too. I walked with a sly smile around my lips. I could not deny the confidence that grew by seeing Mohamed and Ahmed together, most likely talking about me. But I also did not want to return home to disappointment. That their conversation had nothing to do with me.

Sections of the market had fewer people as the sunset came closer to the horizon, but other sections, like the merchants who sold clothes, remained populated despite where the sun was in the sky. I met with a few merchants who sold soccer jerseys. With a few more minutes until sunset and magrib prayer, I left the market and headed home. I never wanted anything more than to return home, and to learn that Ahmed would give me his blessing to leave and search for my parents.

I restrained myself with patience. Ahmed said nothing about his conversation with Mohamed, at least not while I was there. For dinner, Bouchra made oven-cooked chicken and potato fries drenched in sauce; the dish called djaj mhamer. I grabbed a small chair and sat across the table. I occasionally looked at Bouchra and Ahmed. They exchanged a few words here and there but nothing of my interest. Dinner felt longer than usual. I spent every moment hoping Ahmed would speak of his conversation with Mohamed. But it never happened. Bouchra brought apples and bananas after we finished the plate of djaj mhamer.

"You can pursue whatever you want," Ahmed said, to my stunning surprise. I had lost hope by then, but those words widened my eyes and turned my attention toward him. He placed aside his book and faced me. "The last location I know of your parents is that they were in Egypt. That is all. I do not want any more questions. You want to go look for them, go ahead. But no more questions."

Bouchra stood at the ed of the hall, wearing an apron and her hands were wet from washing the dishes. When I met her eyes, she smiled in my direction.

"We will always be here if you decide to return," she said with a gentle tone.

I tried holding the excitement but a wide grin slipped through my lips. I thought about the dream, of my parents. I wanted to jump and hug both of them, Ahmed and Bouchra. But I knew that he would not like it and Bouchra was across the room.

Ahmed continued before I could manage to get any words out of my lips. "But I will warn you now, while Bouchra listens, it is not easy out there. You have to open your eyes and trust no one."

Those words dimmed my excitement. I wondered if that was his goal, to invoke a certain fear. No matter, I was still looking forward to leaving and searching for my parents. The dream ran through my mind again—the water, the crowds of people, the dunes, the sun on the horizon, and my parents sitting with their hands tied. With nothing stopping now, I was certainly going to try. No matter the fear I had, I had to try.

"It will be different," I told them. "But like Bouchra said, I can always return here if I decide otherwise anytime through my journey. Will you accept me?"

"Of course," Bouchra said, immediately.

"Don't ask questions like that," Ahmed said with a serious expression. "You know where we live, you know where my shop is."

At least I had that in case of an emergency. But looking forward, I also expected more obstacles ahead. That day, I removed one obstacle—Ahmed's refusal of me leaving—but more obstacles came ahead, like how I would cross the Sahara Desert to reach Egypt. Though I could not tell from the dream if it were Egypt or Morocco, Ahmed's recent detail about them being in Egypt last, unfortunately made me more certain they were in Egypt than in Morocco. More obstacles appeared ahead. I went out and bought myself cookies and a pomegranate drink called raibi jamila.

That evening, I celebrated for passing through the first obstacle. The other obstacles were tomorrow's problem.

3

On Friday, I said goodbye to my merchant friends. I chose it specifically because Fridays were the shortest workday of the week. Most merchants closed shop between Jummah prayer and Asr prayer—early to late afternoon. About half returned in the evening. I planned to say goodbye before Jummah prayer and not return after Asr prayer, for good.

As for heading to the Sahara Desert, I had plans to either leave that Sunday or, at the latest, Monday morning. I still had no specific plan for crossing the desert, just a piece of paper with some notes. I knew of a few tour groups that traveled from Marrakech to Merzouga. But had no definite information of groups who crossed the desert. I heard from merchants who said there were caravans throughout the year, but nothing with certainty. I planned to ensure I had a few options by tomorrow.

I washed my face and had some time to myself. In the living room, I searched inside my travel backpack. It helped me distance my mind from the worries I carried about things that could go wrong. Who could I turn to if I became sick? What about thieves? Could I withstand the desert heat? All these questions filled my head so that I stopped thinking much about the dream or the minor details like the dripping water at the sink. I turned to the hallway and listened. When I really focused on the dripping and the neighbors and other sounds, they drove those thoughts away.

When Bouchra and Ahmed came into the living room with breakfast, I greeted them and hid my backpack behind the television table. Though I had their blessing to travel, I could not fight off the feeling of guilt. The feeling stemmed from my understanding that I was abandoning them. That they adopted me and raised me and now I planned to leave them for my parents. As I sat there, eating msmen with butter and honey, I considered another idea that I had not thought about until recently. What if my parents left me as a kid for a reason? That they were trying to get rid of me.

I had too much on my mind.

"Is this your last day at the market?" Bouchra asked, pouring more tea into my cup.

The question removed those thoughts and brought me back to reality. "Yes," I told her, and then gestured for only half a cup of tea. Though I faked my appetite when I ate with them, that morning, I had no appetite. "Ahmed will allow me to say goodbye in the morning to the people I know."

"If you decide to return, whenever, you're welcome to."

I nodded with the best smile I could manage. She could tell I had unsettling thoughts on my mind. Even Ahmed had eyes on me, carefully assessing me.

At the market, I visited the merchants I knew. I left the hardest goodbyes at the end—among them, Mohamed. When he came into sight, I saw that he had a lot of people around him, purchasing eggs of different kinds. Mornings were the busiest for him, and I rarely visited him in the mornings, as I had my own work. From afar, I waited as customers left and more customers came. At one point, I considered leaving, not saying goodbye. That he was busy at the time was a sign. I could feel my eyes watering. And then I walked toward him. I would regret if I had left without saying goodbye.

He greeted me with a smile. "Salam, Darius."

"Salam, Uncle Mohamed," I said, and then looked to help. I assisted a lady who had a basket filled with turkey eggs. "I came by to say goodbye, but it seems like you're having a busy morning." I took one hundred dirhams from the lady and handed them to Mohamed. He gave me the change, and I gave it to the lady.

"Praise be to God for that," he said, raising his hands and eyes to the clear sky. "You will be missed, Darius. Many merchants I know speak only well of you. You have taken a different path from kids your age. I am confident that wherever life takes you, you will be great." He turned, giving me his full attention now that there were no more customers. "Always remember where you came from."

I tried my best to hold my tears, but my best was not enough. He leaned over and wrapped his arms around me. It only inflamed my feelings, and I let out another burst of tears.

"Remember, you are in control of your life; no one can decide for you, except you." He unwrapped and held my cheeks with his wrinkly hands, wiping the tears with his thumbs. "Don't forget to visit your second family. I wish you all good things, as you want them."

I wiped my tears, speechless. Mohamed packed three chicken eggs and three turkey eggs into a small plastic bag. His words gave me more confidence. Though the Sahara Desert was like a dark unknown, his words boosted my confidence to a point I felt I could manage it, somehow.

"Here are a few eggs—" he began.

"No, Uncle Mohamed."

"It is disrespectful to refuse a gift," he told me. I took the eggs and hugged him. "Now go on… go see the world and find your parents."

"Thank you, Uncle Mohamed, and thank you for talking with Ahmed the other day." I said and stepped away. He gave me a wink and a firm salute. I gave him my best smile and walked away.

* * *

The following day, I slept in. My imagination kept me awake past midnight; mind occupied with things that could go wrong. I woke to the talking of Ahmed and Bouchra, eating breakfast beside me. I rubbed my eyes and rose to a sitting position. I slept on the sidari—a Moroccan-style couch—perpendicular to where they sat.

Ahmed left for the market, and Bouchra had a friend over to help her with the new rug. It had been almost a year since I had missed the market. It only happened when I became too ill to leave. I ate breakfast in the living room alone. With my appetite, I struggled to complete the two scrambled eggs Bouchra had made for me. I could hear her and her friend gossiping about the neighbors who had left for a vacation in Rabat. Once I had finished the three scrambled eggs, I cleaned the table and washed the dishes. The dishes dried on the rack, and I paused a moment, looking at the dripping water. I tried closing the faucet tighter, but drops continued, one every few seconds.

In the living room, I opened my backpack and unpacked all the items for the third time that week. With limited room, I packed only important items. As for the things that were easily purchasable, I had money. I double-checked again, ensuring that all that I needed was inside. The most important things were money and drafted plan. I looked over the draft plan.

Go from Marrakech to Merzouga through Ouarzazate and Tinghir. It is possible to travel on your own, by bus, or take a tour guide from Marrakech. This is your first phase of travel.

From Merzouga, they have seasonal trips where Bedouins travel across the desert. To cross with them, you have to arrive by a certain date. I will find myself lucky, and the dates that they head out from Merzouga are only weeks away. At least that is what I heard from a travel agency in Marrakech, who frequently take people on trips to Merzouga.

* * *

It wasn't much, but I had plans that day to ask around, specifically about crossing the Sahara Desert. I sat there for a moment, reviewing the notes. I had depended on a lot of things to work out. And more, I had other people on whom I depended, something I did not like doing. I folded the note and tucked it inside the small pocket along with the money I had. I placed more confidence in the money I had. I hoped it would take me across the desert. But part of me doubted it would take me all the way there. I did not know how much it cost to travel across the desert—the agency would not tell me until I booked a tour group with them. And as for the tour group, I went yesterday and asked around. Many of them were eight-hundred dirhams or more. That amount was the local price. I hesitated in booking then, and still did not know if I wanted to go with a tour group. My other option was a bus. But that meant I had to walk some distance or get a ride to the bus stop. The bus would save me a lot of money for the part inside the desert.

Along with the money and the drafted plan, I kept a note of the dream. The dream had changed little. It repeated the same things, and though some nights it repeated more than once, it never repeated more than twice.

With the note in hand, I stared at a particular detail. Ahmed told me they were last known to be in Egypt. I laid my head back on the sidari and stared at the single lightbulb with the electric wire coming out from the wall. My entire life, I thought my parents were Moroccan—Ahmed made it seem so. But at least now, what Ahmed told me aligned with the dream I had. In some ways, it made me feel a type of reassurance, but it also meant the dream must've been true.

Why did my parents have their hands tied and look sorrowfully at me? I thought.

On Sunday, I left the home I knew. I sat with Ahmed during breakfast, forcing myself to eat despite my lack of appetite. Bouchra left no space inside my backpack; she filled it with food.

She placed hard-boiled eggs, sandwiches with olive oil and cheese, pastries, olives, and an assortment of nuts and dates.

That reality of leaving the only home I knew settled in. For the first time, I noticed things I had a luxury of—Bouchra making me breakfast every morning, a job that taught me valuable skills and provided me with an income, a place where I can sleep, two guardians who treated me as if I was their own. All these things, as I ate breakfast that morning, came to my mind. In a few minutes, they would become history. I only hoped that the cost of sacrificing all these blessings was worth the dream I had of my parents.

When I finished breakfast, I wore a clean t-shirt and linen pants. I considered taking a sweatshirt—one of my merchant friends told me that the desert at night became cold. I decided to take it. I made one last check of my bag and then left the living room. Walking through the hall, I could hear Ahmed and Bouchra discussing a rug inside their room. But their voices faded behind my head. Every step I took toward the door felt heavier than the prior one. I turned my head toward the faucet. The dripping sound settled my mind a bit—a familiar sound. It brought the dream to mind. It also gave me the courage to continue forward. I was not traveling without a purpose. My parents waited at the end of my journey, and the journey started with the first step out that door.

I waited at the door with my backpack at my feet. My legs felt heavy; they shook with fear. With the door to my back, I soaked in the small apartment one more time—the kitchen, the narrow hallway, the small bathroom, and Ahmed and Bouchra's bedroom door. A farewell to the only home I knew. My focus turned to my guardians as they stepped out of their room. Bouchra met me with a smile, as usual. Ahmed grunted and held the side of his hip; it still pained him. And the thought of me leaving them pained me mentally. Part of me wanted to unpack my bag and tell him that we're going to the market. But I had to leave. Otherwise, a heavy regret would come crashing down on me later in life.

"This is goodbye," I said, struggling to smile. My words came out shakier than I had expected.

"Do you have everything you need?" Bouchra asked, looking at my backpack. "I tried to pack you as much food as I could. But if you want to return, you're always welcome."

I nodded. I could not find the right words. Ahmed had a bucket hat in his hand. When they were less than a meter away, he handed it to me.

"I want you to have this," he said, his face still expressionless. "You will need it if you're planning on crossing the Sahara Desert."

Last night, I explained my plan to them to find my parents. I told them I had to reach Merzouga first and then from there, hopefully, travel on a caravan across the desert. Bouchra looked worried, and Ahmed seemed unbothered, but beneath that expression, I noticed a feeling of contained emotion. It almost seemed as if he knew I would cross the Sahara Desert. He did not want me to proceed with the plan.

"Thank you, Ahmed," I said, taking the bucket hat. I hugged them both, cried a bit, and then stepped out the door before my eyes unleashed more tears. I found the best way to escape feelings was to step out of the situation that brought those feelings on. With the backpack on my back and the bucket hat on my head, I started my adventure to find my parents.

When I stepped outside, out into the warm sun and the sounds of neighbors talking, I had a new sense of feeling in my heart. It made me stop and think. Moments ago, I feared what would come and worried that things might happen the way I wanted them to. But as I stood there, thinking about this feeling, my mind seemed to look forward to the adventure. It was as if it craved the novelty of the adventures that lay ahead. I smiled and sauntered away.

I took out the paper with the notes and reviewed the plan ahead.

It had been my guide, the paper with small notes. I went to tour agencies and researched most of Friday evening and Saturday. The first step was to leave the outskirts of Marrakech and then travel through the mountain range—the High Atlas Mountains—to reach Rissani and then Merzouga. But I would not travel through the mountains on foot. It would take too long. And time had not been on my side. The thought of that young girl crossed my mind, the one Bouchra told me about. And then the image of my parents on their knees with their hands tied. The dream remained the same the last few nights, so in one respect, I felt confident that things were still fine.

Our town was on the outskirts of Marrakech. I could either return to Marrakech and take the bus from there, or walk a few kilometers to the next stop. On the plan, I noted that it was better that I walked to the next stop rather than go back to Marrakech and take it from there. I walked on the dirt path of a large road. With only a few minutes into the trip, I was happy that everything had worked out my way. A gust of wind caught me by surprise and almost blew off my bucket hat. I smiled as it came suddenly. Though the hat flew off my head, the string kept it holstered around my neck.

As I walked, I occupied my mind with the market. I thought of my merchant friends, wondering what they were doing. I looked at my wristwatch, a small one that Ahmed had given me years ago. At eleven in the morning, I typically sat outside the shop, trying to bring customers into our shop. It had been the time tourists populated the market.

A car horn startled me. I turned, and the driver waved me over.

"Sorry," I waved to him. I walked too close to the street. Seeing the cars drive down, it presented me with an idea. Instead of walking all six or seven kilometers, I could try to get a ride from a local. It was worth trying. If being a merchant taught me anything, it was convincing others to my goals. I raised my left thumb and occasionally turned, hoping to grab a driver's attention. A few minutes later, my arm became tired and so I gave up.

My stomach rumbled for food. I had an appetite to eat anything, and to eat a lot. Walking further away from the road, I found a small rock and used it as a seat. I dropped my bag at the side and searched through the food that Bouchra had packed for me. She packed four sandwiches and five hard-boiled eggs.

Thank you, Bouchra, I thought. I had a plastic water bottle with me. I drank about halfway through.

Once I had satisfied my stomach with food, I tucked the water bottle back into my backpack and the plastic wrap, and then continued onward. I held my thumb up and continued walking. To my luck, a car drove slowly nearby and then honked. I looked at the road.

A man peeked out of the passenger window. "Do you need a ride somewhere ahead?"

I smiled and rushed toward the car. "Yes, uncle, if that will not be troublesome." As the man had leveled me, I also leveled him. Picking up a stranger on the road was not good for the person being picked up and the person who was driving. It brought its risks for both parties. But I wore my best smile and easy expression—the one I usually wore when I met customers in front of the shop and wanted them to purchase our rugs. So I hoped the man would know that I am a good person. From my end, the man looked presentable in a dress shirt and drove a small Dacia. To me, the man looked safe to drive with.

"I am heading that way, and depending on how dar you have to go, you can come along. It is almost noon, and it is not safe to walk in the sun at this time."

"Thank you, Uncle. I am heading to the bus stop for the buses that are going to Rissani and Merzouga."

The man nodded. "That's not too far along. You weren't walking from Marrakech, were you?"

"No," I turned to where I came from, "I'm coming from the nearby town."

He waved me into the car. "I can drop you off there. I am heading to Ouarzazate, so it's on the way there."

I opened the door and entered his car. The man was right. The sun rose in the sky, and it had been boiling compared to around noon time at the market. Outside there, there was nothing to cover the sun's direct hit. I placed the bag beside my feet and removed my bucket hat, but kept its string around my neck.

The man extended his hand, "My name is Simo."

"Darius," I said, shaking his hand.

"I like your name," he said, and looked at the side mirror to enter the road fully.

For a few seconds, we drove in silence. He had the air conditioner running, and it felt nice on my skin. It made me realize how hot it must have been outside, even though I had thought little about it. Everything had worked so far, and I could not have been happier. I broke the silence between us and talked to the man about the first thing that came to my mind.

"It feels much hotter here than at the market," I said, looking over to Simo. "When I spent time at the market, I didn't notice the heat, or maybe the sun is more powerful here because there is more open space—little trees, few buildings, and a flat stretch of land. But I should be more careful of the sun and the heat."

I took out my piece of paper and talked a lot about my trip and my life as a merchant. Simo listened and occasionally looked my way. I could feel that sense of happiness in me I rarely felt. It made me talk more than I normally did, and I shared some things that I might have not shared with someone I had just met. My feelings spoke for me, without the words going through my head. I stopped talking when we were a few hundred meters from the bus stop.

"You are a happy person," Simo told me. "But it is not good to be very happy like that. I am happy that you are traveling and that it is your first time. But whenever you are happy, remember to say one thing: Alhamdulillah. What you are feeling right now, a weird type of happiness that comes in a rush, I have felt a few times in my life. It is unlike the others, right?" I nodded as I picked my bag up from near my legs onto my lap. He continued as he stopped the car beside the road. "Just something to keep in mind. I wish you the best during your travels, Darius. Good luck."

As I was about to open the small section of my bag, he placed his hand as to stop me. "It is not necessary. I was driving through here anyway."

"Thank you, Simo." I smiled and opened the door. We shook hands goodbye, and I left his car with sudden haste. In the near distance, I could see a few groups gathered in front of the bus terminal. The first thing I did was look at my watch, but the sudden temperature change distracted me. The car had been much colder than outside. A warm breeze and the penetrating sun differed from what I had become accustomed to at the market. And then I diverted my attention to my watch, curious as to why so many people waited so early. It struck me: I had not been early for that bus; the early bus still hadn't left.

I slung my backpack over one shoulder, held my bucket hat on my head, and ran to the ticket store. From the pack of travelers, I noticed two men who seemed like they were not travelers. They had no luggage near them; they talked to each other and occasionally searched near the taxi stop. It gave me hope; maybe there were more spots on the early bus.

"Excuse me, uncle," I said, coming to an abrupt stop near the men. "Is there still room for—"

"Where are you going?" A man interrupted; on one hand, he played with some coins, and a stack of bills.

"Merzouga," I told him. The man's tone caught me by surprise. In a situation like that, I thought he would speak more kindly. It was what I had been accustomed to at the market. The merchants treated the customers' kindness as if it were the best technique to maintain customers. But in this case, it had been the other way around.

"Three hundred dirhams. One spot left for someone traveling

to Merzouga. It will arrive anytime now, and if you don't take this one, you'll have to wait a couple of hours."

Despite the poor attitude, I got a fair price from him. The price, when I asked people at the market, told me it would get me to Merzouga. But more importantly, anything below nine hundred dirhams had been worth my time. Tours were nine hundred and more. Not only that, but they would have two days before arriving at Merzouga. In hours, and with only three hundred dirhams, the bus would arrive at Merzouga.

In another part of me, I desired to bargain for the price. Not because of the amount, but because it was the right thing to do from a merchant-customer relationship. Merchants always expected the customer to bargain over the price. As a merchant, I would look unusually at a customer who did not bargain, except for the tourists. They never bargained, or rarely successfully. In that situation, seeing the man's expression and hearing the bus arrive, I kept quiet and turned my backpack around.

I froze in place when I saw the small pocket open. I did a quick search and immediately knew what was missing. The papers with the plan. I made a fist and hit it against my other palm. I turned around, hoping for the best outcome—I forgot to close the small pocket and it flew out. There was no paper nearby. I left Simo's car in a hurry; it must've dropped when I picked my bag up.

"Three hundred dirhams; the bus is here."

I counted the three hundred dirhams and then made sure the small pocket was closed. I handed the man the amount and waited for my ticket. The second man tore a ticket and wrote something on it, and then handed it to me.

When the bus parked, men and women rushed near the luggage latch. The driver left the bus and greeted the two men with tickets. He opened then went to open the luggage latch. I had no luggage, so I stood waiting at the door.

"Go on," the man who gave me the ticket said. "We will tell him where you will stop, and your ticket also says your final destination."

I peeked at the note and nodded toward the man. Losing the paper had really dimmed my feelings; they suddenly crashed from the drive earlier. I could not speak to anyone. I remembered what Simo had told me about being too happy. In my mind, I thought, what should I say if it were the opposite? I went up the three steps aboard with heavy legs. The bus had been half-full. I found the closest open seat to the driver and took it for myself. Most people sat on the left side; I found it unusual at first and then remembered that the sun had something to do with that. Thankfully, there were curtains on the windows. I sat near the window, hugged my bag around my chest, and placed my head against the window. I cried quietly to let out the frustration of losing the plan.

4

The bus departed shortly thereafter. I had no other option than to continue my journey forward. If I had turned then, it would have felt like a major loss even when I hadn't traveled over ten kilometers from Ahmed's home. So I continued, and the longer I thought about it, the more I realized it hadn't been a complete loss in the sense of losing the plan paper. It had some notes and ideas of what caravans I could take, but it wasn't a major setback. I had hoped that people, when I arrived at Merzouga, would be truthful about the trips that crossed the desert and about their price.

When the bus got on the road, the sun was hitting my side of the window. I pulled the window curtain and then laid my head against it. A man, about middle age, sat near me. He stank of sweat that made me nauseous for a few minutes. I gave him a long look, not wanting to tell him. Seconds later, he turned and gave me a hard look. It made me look the other way. I knew his type. A person who had nothing to lose; his face had knife cuts and his clothing was unclean. With a t-shirt, his large biceps were on display. I kept to myself and did not think about talking to him. Patience with the scent had been better for me than getting into a confrontation with him. People like him came about the market from time to time, holding a large knife and seeking to fight with anyone they came across.

I laid my head on the curtain against the window and closed my eyes. It had been the first time I had dreamt of my parents during the daytime. But the one thing that had been different was that they were vivid. I could see my parents more clearly than before. I had a similar facial structure to my father. High cheekbones, brown eyes, straight hair, and large lips. My mother had light hazel eyes, and she wore a hijab and had a small nose. Though they became more vivid, the other details of the dream remained the same. The invisible water falling, the sand dunes in the back, and the enormous crowds behind my parents. But this time, the large crowds were not taking pictures; rather, they were carrying something—it seemed like a sack of items. I wanted to focus on what they carried, but a bump on the road made me shift and hit my head against the window. I woke from the dream.

I rubbed my eyes and then looked out the window. We were still carving through the mountains, slowly and safely. It had been a narrow, two-way road. I could not tell where we were, nor how far until we reached Ouarzazate. If I had taken the seat on the other side—the right side of the bus—there were sometimes small pillars on the side of the road with how many kilometers until the next city.

With more details of the dream, I took out a pen and the paper with the notes of the dream. I snuck my money back into the small pocket when I took the paper out. I wrote the details of my parents and of the groups of people behind them. Even when I focused hard on the dream, I could not guess what the people were carrying—whether it really was sacks or something else.

The man beside me had eyes on me as I tucked the note inside. He held a heavy gaze on me as I closed the zipper; I looked his way for a moment. I could not hold his gaze; I was afraid that he would become confrontational.

I leaned back against the window and closed my eyes, both arms wrapped around my bag. For a while, it had been just closing my eyes and thinking of my next move when the bus arrived in Merzouga. But then I fell asleep without the dream.

The bus came to a stop, and I woke up from my nap. The driver parked beside the road, similar to where I had boarded, and then stood at the alley of seats. "Ouarzazate," he called.

My entire life I had never traveled further than Marrakech; at least I do not remember traveling far. Since I could remember, I had lived with Ahmed and Bouchra in that same apartment. I spent my time at their home until I could walk and talk, and then Ahmed started bringing me to the market. Years later, I sold like any other merchant. But I had never traveled further than Marrakech. I looked out the window as some passengers left the bus.

Ouarzazate homes had a reddish-brown hue, similar to Marrakech, but they were made of clay and adobe bricks. They had flat roofs and high walls. It blended really well with the colors of the Sahara Desert. A merchant in Marrakech told me about the city when I told him I was traveling to Merzouga. It had been famous, with tourists visiting it as they visited Marrakech. Another told me it had been the door to the Sahara Desert. I didn't believe him at first, arguing that it had been kilometers from the desert. And that if a city had been considered the entrance, it would surely have been Merzouga or Rissani or Erfoud or any of those cities near the sand dunes. But what he said finally made sense to me.

The bus left the stop after a few minutes of passengers getting off, new ones boarding, and others using the restrooms. We traveled through the city, and it made sense. Ouarzazate had been the gateway to the desert. It sat right between the High Atlas Mountains and the Sahara Desert. We completed the narrow, wiggly roads of the mountains, and now the flat and hazy roads ahead awaited us.

I pulled out more food. It had been past two in the afternoon. I ate a hard-boiled egg and a sandwich. I had only a little water left. With a full stomach and nowhere to go, I laid my head against the window and closed my eyes.

A dozen passengers were left when we arrived in Merzouga, the small town right before the entrance. The man who sat beside me had left somewhere between Ouarzazate and Merzouga. I went down the steps and left the air-conditioned bus. The heat was choking, making the air difficult to breathe. A few passengers went to collect their bags, but I walked away. The sun touched the horizon and gave off beautiful light in the sky above. As I walked to what I thought was the center of Merzouga, I looked back at all that had happened that day. It was a long day, no doubt. But I learned and explored so many things that I hadn't in my entire sixteen years of life.

In the far distance, I spotted the large sand dunes. And as we were close to Merzouga, I noticed a few camels around. It had been my first time seeing them. The thought of not seeing chickens anymore made me hungry. Though I had some food left, I wanted to eat some sort of meat. It had been the first thing I searched for, and I treated it as a treat. Despite a few bumps, I traveled out of Marrakech and was about to travel into the desert. It had been a huge accomplishment, something I had been proud of.

I thought about saving money and resorting to a small stall in the market. They sold chicken and kefta sandwiches. Minced meat was my favorite, as well as Ahmed's. The thought reminded me of years ago when we had eaten those sandwiches in the evening. Bouchra loved chicken, and Ahmed loved putting bits of kefta into her sandwich, tricking her into eating the kefta too. Those were wonderful memories, and they made me smile as I headed for the market.

A well-lit shop caught my eye near the entrance to the market. It had two customers, which wasn't a good sign—popular shops had more customers. But a sign that said, *we welcome all: young, old, magribi, or foreigners*. I looked in what I thought was the direction of the market. It had been late, almost magrib time. Back home, around this time, Ahmed and I would be in the living room eating dinner. My legs hurt from sitting for so long.

With all those, I decided I would treat myself at this shop.

I entered, and a lady warmly greeted me. "Salam, young man. We don't have chicken anymore, but there is still some kefta if you're thinking of ordering the sandwich."

She wore a blue dress that covered her body and parts of her hair. The Saharan Moroccans had different clothing styles than, say, someone from Marrakech or someone from central Morocco or northern Morocco. I also picked up on her slight accent, and I was certain she would when I spoke too.

"That would be perfect. A kefta sandwich, fries, and..." I looked at the glass counter. They had a selection of sodas and fruit drinks. "A poms." It was an apple soda. In that moment, I felt rebellious. Ahmed spoke against drinking sodas. I sometimes snuck outside and had a soda with a sandwich, either at the market or after we closed our shop. Despite his not being there with me, I still felt him watching me, just like the times I've done it in Marrakech, even though we were hundreds of kilometers away.

"You're not from here, are you?"

"No, I'm traveling from Marrakech."

"A great city," a man said from behind the counter. It was her husband. He was putting on cooking gloves. "I lived there for ten years, but then I returned to Merzouga as the city became swarmed by tourists. It's a lot calmer here and we have the Sahara Desert. It has its downsides, but it's great to have the ability to walk out in the desert and relax by the dunes— especially at night."

"I am thinking of traveling across the desert," I said, putting my bag down so I could take my money out. "How much is a kefta sandwich with fries and a can of poms?"

"Thirty-six dirhams," she said, "but the sandwich is filled with kefta."

I had paused briefly before opening the zipper. Compared to Marrakech, the prices were higher. But I also thought about the cost of bringing all the items to Merzouga. It seemed like the further one was away from Casablanca and central Morocco, the more money things became, except for local items. A few merchants told me about this when I visited them, particularly the clothing merchants. They brought clothes from Casablanca, and so the cost rose with distance. I continued on to open the zipper on my money.

My heart dropped.

My stack of money was not there. I began to panic, opening the large pocket and the place where I had a change of clothes. Nothing. I could feel my head become light. Fear sank deep into my thoughts. I searched my pockets. Without money, I could not travel, whether it was forward or backward. Without money, I had no food or drink. I tried retracing my steps, thinking about how I had lost my money. And then it came to me. The man sitting next to me on the bus. He saw me taking money out. I occasionally fell asleep, and stayed with me beyond Ouarzazate, less than an hour from Merzouga. I wanted to beat myself up.

"What is wrong? What did you lose?" The man asked, worried.

I looked beside her and addressed him, "Don't make the sandwich, please. I don't have the money to pay for it."

The couple looked at each other for a long while. I closed my bag and started to head out the door. My legs felt heavy, and I had to put my hand on my head because of the lightheadedness I felt. At one point, I wanted to stop and lie down to rest. But I also did not want to bother them. I looked at the door and pushed myself to leave first and then collapsed on the ground. I had not known the lady was talking to me until she tapped my shoulder. I turned to her.

"We said you can stay and have the meal," the lady said. "If you lost your money, then you have bigger problems to deal with. You should deal with them on a full stomach. Take a seat, young man, and we'll get your food ready in a few minutes."

I stood there for a moment; she did too, but then she left. I was speechless, but I think she knew how appreciative I was for them to allow me to eat for free. I took the closest seat I could find and then placed my bag near my feet. I placed my head on the table for a moment, unsure of what I was going to do now that I had no money.

The sandwich had so much minced meat and spices. The fries were warm, at best, but I never complained for a free meal. I wanted to tell them that the pom soda was not necessary, that the food they gave me was more than enough, but the man insisted and kept the can on the table. The lady was right. A stomach with food made the situation better. Though I still had to figure something out, I had some ideas. In that moment, the idea of traveling across the desert was out of the question. I had no money and no time. Whatever were to happen to my parents, I had to accept their fate. I felt terrible, but circumstances made the choice.

"How was the food?" the man asked as he came around to collect the empty plate on which the only things on it were some ketchup and bread crumbs.

"Amazing," I told him. "Please forgive me for not having money. I swear, I didn't know until now. May Allah reward you and your wife with something better than the cost of the meal."

"You paid us, young man," he said. "That prayer is worth more than the thirty-six dirhams you would have given us. Now, about your situation." He took the plate and empty soda can and walked to the glass counter, dropped them off and walked back. "I have a friend. He is a shop owner, but at the market, who might need help from time to time. I know you said you're planning to travel inside the desert with the caravans, but considering that you have no more money, I think your plan is not good, right?"

I nodded. In my mind, if I had enough money to return to Marrakech, I would take the next bus out tomorrow. But his mention of a shop owner gave me more ideas. I listened to him closely, with wide eyes at the words he might say next.

"Our markets are usually full on certain days," he continued, cleaning his hands on the apron he wore. "Unlike your markets that are full most days, if not all days of the week. I know someone who might need help on a few days of the week. I am not sure if he still does, but it is worth a shot considering your situation. He will treat you well and he will pay you a fair amount for your work. Would you be interested?"

At the moment, I did not know whether that would be the right choice. The moment he said shop owner, I knew that he would say something like that. It had been common for young kids to learn trades, such as being a merchant or mechanic; we called it "sell and buy." The whole situation of losing my travel notes and money really dimmed my desire to travel and seek out the dream, no matter its consequences. Especially when all these unfortunate events happened within the first day. I could only expect more things ahead, particularly in the depths of the Sahara Desert.

"I am actually a merchant," I told him. He sat on the seat across from me. "I worked for a few years with my guardian. We have a rug shop."

The man gestured with both hands toward me. "That is perfect. Maktub. Though I do not know exactly if my friend there needs help at this time; it is not August or July, where tourism is high, but if you ask him, he might direct you to another merchant in the market that might need help with selling or something else that would pay you enough money to continue onward with your trip."

"Uncle, I am not sure if I want to continue," I said these words with a heavy heart. Even my own body would not accept those words. "I had some other unfortunate events happen today that make me think that if I continue, I will lose myself by the end of the adventure." I paused because he was shaking his head with passion.

He leaned forward, placed both forearms on the table, and looked me straight in the eyes. "I do not know you well, young man, but if there is one thing you can take from me, is that you must continue onward. Of course, I do not know your complete story, but moving forward, in my honest opinion, is the best thing you can do. Life has multiple obstacles, and we will all go through them, but you do not know what awaits you ahead. I will share with you a story." He turned and asked his wife for a glass of water. She brought me a glass of water, too.

"My wife and I met solely by chance," he said after taking the first drink. "You know the festival with the horses? When the men line up in a straight line, with rifles in hand, they kick their horses forward for a few seconds, and just before they reach the end, they try to shoot into the sky at the same time. Ten to fifteen men shooting at the same time so that it comes out as if only one shot."

I nodded. I had never attended those festivals, but I know Ahmed did years ago. He talked about them a few times when he shared his old memories.

The man continued. "My friend and I went to these events as kids. My motorcycle would not work that day. I became extremely upset with myself and my motorcycle. When my friend came over, I told him I would no longer go because my motorcycle was not working. He insisted, but I refused. We exchanged some heated words, especially from me. I apologized after, of course. Then he told my mother at the time—he was a close family friend, always over our house for meals, or I went to his home for meals.

"So then my mother got involved. We went to the festival on his motorcycle, even though it had been small. When we arrived, we enjoyed our time. But I honestly was still upset with my motorcycle not working. I saw this beautiful girl from a distance. But her beauty wasn't the only thing that caught my eye; something else did too."

The man took another sip; I did too, and continued listening attentively to his story. I loved hearing stories, and that was partly why I loved walking around our market. Older men, especially, had great stories to tell. I could see at the back counter his wife listening to the story as well, smiling with her eyes and lips.

"I told my friend about the girl," he continued. "And he pushed me to go up to her family. I did not want to, not because I saw no future with her, but because I was too nervous. If you knew my friend, you'd know that he does not give up easily. He continued, and we finally went up to the family. He initially talked on my behalf; I stayed half a meter away. I got their number, my family met theirs, and I got the most amazing woman.

"What I am trying to say with all this is that you do not know what life has in store for you. Now imagine if I had not gone that day because of my motorcycle. An obstacle comes your way, deal with that obstacle, maneuver around it. But do not give up because you do not know what awaits on the other side."

"You're right…" I said, thinking of my parents. I had not told him about them, nor why I was traveling across the desert. But if he knew my reason, I was sure the man would have fervently pushed me to continue, as his friend did years ago. "I will have to ask your friend about some job in the market. Thankfully, I have some expertise in selling. Like you said, maybe this is God's plan. Maktub."

I had been familiar with the work. The first time I heard it was from a merchant who was teaching it to a group of tourists in the market. I was very young.

"Maktub," he repeated. "Go to him tomorrow. I will call him either early tomorrow or later tonight so that he knows you're coming."

I thought more of that word as I prepared to sleep that night. The man did not want to let me leave. He insisted I spend the night at his home. But I kindly refused. We finally agreed that I'd spend the night at his restaurant. He took me to a small room in the back and brought me a floor mat and bedsheets from his home.

And then he left with his wife and told me he'd return early the next morning, at around seven. I could not thank him enough for all he had done for me. But I also saw that all he had done was written. The likelihood of meeting the person who'd set me up with a merchant at the market.

The following morning I woke with new details of the dream. Unlike the girl Bouchra had told me about, the dream did not become more horrifying. The first thing I did was take out the note of my dreams. I had very little space left and so I tried including the details in small writing.

Since the start of the dreams, this one had been the most vivid. I could see things very clearly. The people behind my parents were carrying sacks of grain; my parents' faces became clearer. But still, I could not confirm if it were them. I had been too young when I was last with them, but from their facial details, I resembled each of them, particularly my father. And among the newest details of the dream was the robe I was wearing. In the dream, I had looked down at myself, wearing long robes, and quite expensive ones. On the left chest area, I noticed a pin of sorts, but I had raised my head before I could really get a glimpse of it entirely.

I sat on the floor mat, looking out near the door. I thought of the dream, wondering if I had missed any details. It had already slipped out of my mind. If only I could have heard a noise within the dream, that would have made the dream more interesting. Overall, as I tucked the note back inside the small pocket, I labeled this dream as a good sign. That, somehow, I should continue onward with the journey.

But how can I without any money, I thought. The caravan would have to depart in a few days, and I knew for certain I would not have enough money to leave with the upcoming one. I did not know when the next one would be.

The nights and early mornings were noticeably colder than the days. I folded the bedsheets and made the place look tidy for when Brahim arrived that morning. I sat waiting for him, without a thing to do. If I hadn't promised him I would stay, I would have already left in search of breakfast. But I wanted to stay, and so I waited until seven in the morning. It arrived, and I continued waiting. He arrived at half-past seven. I, a foreigner, might have been upset with the delayed arrival, but I was a Moroccan and he was too; being on schedule had not been our norm.

At about nine in the morning, I started my way to the market. Brahim had not taken the floor mat and the bedsheets. I left his shop, hoping that he would allow me to stay another night. He considered telling him if I could, or at least to do it subtly. To ask him if I could keep my bag in his shop until I returned that night. There was no simple path to ask him, and so I left, thanking him for all he had done for me since last night without pushing my luck.

The market in Merzouga had a different atmosphere compared to the one I had been used to. But it had been a Moroccan market. Markets were my second home, or maybe at that point, my only home as I had no other home. I walked in with a puff of the chest and a skip in my step. It was more confidence than arrogance.

Brahim told me about his friend, a spice merchant. But he told me not to raise my hopes too high. He called him last night and told him he didn't need help, but I was welcome to visit and he would talk to me directly. I searched for the spice section of the market. Most shops were open, but the market lacked customers. I easily found the spice section—the market had been a fraction of the size of our market.

I walked from Brahim's shop, disappointed. He thanked me for my interest and said that I was welcome in the summer, but there were too few customers for him to need someone besides himself. I went back to square one. No money and no way of getting money. I walked with my head down for a few minutes, thinking about what I should do. I raised my head and lifted my shoulders. I could not allow one merchant to tell me there was no work to make me give up. I raised my head and lifted my shoulders. If I had to ask everyone at the market for a job, I had to do it.

And so for the next couple of hours, I went to all the merchants in the market and asked them for a job at their shop. I sold myself well, sharing details of my expertise. Initially, they looked at me curiously and cautiously. A young man who knew the trade of selling. They did not believe it. I did not blame them. Though each time I visited a merchant and they kindly declined to take me as their assistant, I became more upset and determined to find one merchant. I left each shop telling myself that I would not leave the market until I had asked every merchant with a shop.

I literally went to every shop. I stood near the last one. A fabric merchant. He was with a client, so I waited until he finished. He wore nice clothes, a dress shirt and linen pants. Unlike most merchants, he looked very wealthy. I thought maybe that was the reason of him wearing wealthy clothing—he was a fabric merchant.

"What can I do you for?" the man walked to me as the customers were leaving the shop.

"It's good fabric," I said to the customers walked beside him. They gave me a look and continued on their way. I wanted to share with them the origin of the fabric, but I was not certain. I thought it best that I kept my mouth closed, as it could ruin my reputation with the merchant if I spoke the wrong location. I turned to the merchant. "My name is Darius. I'm from Marrakech and looking for a job in this market." After those words, this was where I lost about half the merchants' interest. But the fabric merchant heard me out. "I am an experienced merchant. I planned to travel on a trip to the Sahara Desert, but someone stole my money before I arrived in Merzouga. Now I have no money to return to Marrakech or continue onward. I literally asked everyone, all the merchants who are here today, but no one has a job for a merchant like me. Please." I wanted to drop to my knees and beg him.

The man wore a pleasant fragrance, one of the Arabian fragrances. I wanted to comment on the fragrance, a compliment, but I held it for the time. I waited his response. I had followups ready, such as the compliment, but as a merchant, I knew speaking too much might divert the person you are trying to sell to. And though I was not selling the fabric merchant anything physical, I was trying to sell him myself, convince him I was worthy of working with him.

He leveled me for a long moment; it felt close to a minute without neither of us talking. I allowed him to think, but I reached a point where I looked away, as if studying his array of fabrics.

"My name is Ishaq," he said extending a hand. We shared a firm handshake. "You said that you asked *all* the merchants in the market?"

"Yes, all who are here today. Some shops are closed, or at least might have been closed when I walked by them."

"Come with me," he waved me out his shop.

I followed him. My backpack had felt heavy on my shoulders. I held the straps, knowing what he planned to do. It was a test, and I knew I would pass. For the next five minutes, we walked around the market, and he randomly asked merchants if I had talked to them. All of them said yes. We returned to his shop.

"You are a truthful person from what I can tell," he said, taking a white plastic seat from the back and putting it near a stack of boxes near the back. And then, pointing to the chair, he said, "Put your backpack here. I want to see your merchandising skills. Show me how good you are with the next—" He looked over me and smiled. He adjusted his round glasses on the edge of his nose. "This is your opportunity. Help those customers who walked in."

I turned to find a couple standing a meter away, searching the fabric rolls. Uncertainty settled onto my stomach. It was not the on-the-spot situation of selling fabric, it had been more of the situation would either grant me the position or it would lead to me walking without a job. So much weight fell on my shoulders to preform. I took a deep breath and performed as if they were buying rugs from Ahmed's shop. I had to strut my expertise; no merchant asked me to sell their merchandise to other customers.

I started strong, using all the experience I have learned from the past ten years with Ahmed. But it took only a couple minutes of speaking with them for me to realize they weren't the type of customers who were trying to make a purchase. We merchants called these customers, just searching around for prices. If they were to really purchase, they would walk around the entire market before making a purchase. I tried giving them a great offer, and spoke with them with many smiles, but I lacked on thing that I had back in Marrakech. I did not know the value red line of the fabrics—the lowest price we could sell them for a profit. For this reason, I gave them I fair price, based on what Ishaq said, but he would not tell me that detail of the red line.

Still, I tried to get them to purchase without knowing the final price. I turned the conversation away from the price and the quality of the fabric. I mentioned where it came from and said good things about the fabric—most details I had made up. Still, it had not been enough for them to purchase. And honestly, I thought it had more to do with the fact that they were not planning to buy that morning than with my expertise.

When they left, I turned to Ishaq with a disappointed expression. The only shot I had, I could not seal the deal. But his expression raised my spirits. He nodded to himself slowly, looking at me with satisfied eyes.

"You clearly know the basics," he said. "Whether you have worked for ten years or a few years, I am impressed for the skill that you have at your age. How old are you?"

"Nineteen, sir. Almost twenty."

Ishaq nodded and rose from his seat. "The customers weren't

trying to buy any fabric. They were only looking around, trying to see what fabric was available in the market. They might return, but they might not. It had not been your fault that you had not sold to them. No matter how experienced a merchant could be, if the customer enters with a mind of not buying, it is hard, not impossible, but very hard to change their mind. This is what I will do with you. I will allow you to help me this week, starting today. It will give me time to see how good you really are and in return I will pay you a small commission. Does that sound like a plan you're willing to proceed with?"

"Yes, sir. I will appreciate that a lot." I said those words but really, I wanted to drop and cry tears of happiness. It had not been a set deal, but I had something when earlier that morning, I had nothing. Even if things went bad, a week's worth might give me enough money to travel part of the way back to Marrakech.

A week later, I left Ishaq's shop with enough money to return to Marrakech. I spent the last week sleeping at Brahim's restaurant; thankfully he allowed me to stay until I had enough money. And I ate only two meals a day, to save as much money as possible. So I walked that evening, wondering if I wanted to leave for Marrakech the following day or, as Ishaq had offered, spent the next few weeks leading his shop and making even more money to travel across the desert.

I missed the caravan I planned to take, I thought.

But I had another option, to take the caravan leaving Merzouga in about six or seven weeks. It would provide me time to gather more money. And as of for the dream, it had not concerned me. It remained the same, unlike what happened to the girl Bouchra told me about. I had no nightmares; and most of the details I had seen were vivid. I also thought about Brahim and Mohamed's words, how they pushed me to proceed with my trip. I had told Brahim one evening. Once I told him about the dream and my parents and my upbringing with Ahmed and Bouchra, he became more insistent that I continue with my journey. So much, that he allowed me to spend nights at his shop.

I was headed there when, just before leaving the market, noticed a young man, about my age, drop an envelope. It fell from his back pocket. The young man walked in a rapid pace, just short of a jog. I picked the envelope off the ground and followed him. As I tried remove the dirt from the envelope, I noticed the blue two hundred bills, many of them. The envelope was thick with money.

Who could stop me if I were to take the envelope and walk the opposite direction, I thought. I shook my head from that thought and ran to him. I tapped his back shoulder and extended the hand with the envelope. I could have taken the money.

The young man tapped his back pockets and took the envelope. "Thank you so much. Oh my, the shop owner would have been very upset with me." To my surprise, he leaned and wrapped me in a hug. "I wish I could pay you back. Thank you. Thank you."

"Don't worry about it," I said with a smile, shaking it off. "I am sure that you would have done the same if the roles were opposite."

"Yes, of course. Of course." The young man searched through his pockets, trying to find a place best to keep the envelope. "My name is Adam, by the way." He placed it between his waist and pants, tying the string around his waist tight. He looked up and extended a hand for a handshake.

"My name is Darius," I said, his face clicking in my memory. I had met him briefly before, the first day at the market. He was selling spices when I asked to the shop owner for available work.

"Nice to meet you, Darius. I will see you around!" He said the last statement while turning, and running through the market's gates.

I thought about the money during the walk to the restaurant.

The Merchant's Dream

5

Weeks later, I anticipated the upcoming caravan trip starting from Merzouga. I talked to a few people about it. They confirmed a second caravan left from Merzouga before the end of the year.

Since meeting Adam and got the job at Ishaq's, I lived in Adam's apartment. It had been a small apartment, but enough for the two of us. I paid him half the amount, and it gave me a place to stay the nights. We also became very close friends. Days before the caravan trip, I told Adam that I was leaving in a few days.

"A caravan trip across the desert?" He looked at me with intriguing eyes. I noticed that my statement spark certain interest in his eyes.

"Yes, I… well, I'm trying to cross the desert to Egypt for something; it awaits me over there." I hesitated on telling him the full truth. I noticed that many people in the area did not support the idea of me traveling across the desert. Brahim was the only person. Everyone else thought it had been a bad idea to cross the desert, and that most people who did were out of their minds, had a real reason to enter the desert, or were tourists also out of their minds. For that reason, I stopped telling people about my dream.

"What is this thing that awaits you?"

"I would rather not say."

Adam gave me a look, but did not push for more details. He locked the apartment door, and we walked to the market that morning.

"It happens that I have always wanted to cross the Sahara Desert. It has been a lifelong goal of mine to cross it and possibly see the pyramids." Adam leaned over close to me and whispered. "I hope to find treasure in the pyramids and make myself rich. Ouuu I would love that. Gold, diamonds, jewelry. I will become the richest person in Africa."

I looked into his eyes; they lit up with his words. He paused a moment, possibly daydream of his future wealth. It had been the first time he displayed to me his love for riches and wealth. When we lived together, we occasionally ate outside. He would spend money freely without be a stingy person.

"What made you not go?"

"It's dangerous, or so I heard," Adam broke off from his daydreaming and wore a disappointed expression. "Are you certain you want to cross the desert? I mean, it could kill you. You might die. People die on these journeys. The heat is the Sahara's deadliest killer, and then there are scorpion and snake bites, sandstorms, and ongoing clan battles, and so much more. Not everyone survives. So whatever reason you want to visit Egypt, it should be worth the trip."

Those words made me fearful of what would happen. I also thought there were risks in anything with life. Even selling in the market had its worries—whether a merchant would sell on a certain day, people stealing items, a drunk person ruining the products.

I turned around and looked at the sand dunes. They were visible from anywhere in Merzouga. I could die in the Sahara Desert. It really made me think whether all this was worth the journey to Egypt. All for a dream. A dream I did not know whether it had truth; what it truly meant. And even if I were to live, there was a possibility I would find nothing on the other side of the sand dunes.

The dream came to me again, the sand dunes behind my parents, where the crowds were, near the pyramids. They were the sand dunes in my dream. Part of me wanted to give all this up, seeing that my life was on the line while I might not achieve what I set out for, but also part me would not accept giving up with all the weeks I have spent in Merzouga and all the trouble I had endured so far.

I could not give up.

"You know, I have tried multiple times. I tried going last, but I froze when I saw the large groups of people preparing themselves. I also tried a few months ago and a few weeks ago." Adam shook his head. "Every time I get closer. But in the end, I never make the commitment to continue onward."

"Come with me," I said. "We will have each other as support."

Adam looked hesitant. He turned away from me, toward the market, and said, "I will think about it today and let you know."

Four days later, Adam and I were packing our items. He had to throw away a lot of his clothes so that he could leave with only a backpack. I bought a few water bottles, nuts, dates, and snacks. I fit as much as I could into my bag and then I added more to a small bag I would hold with one hand. With so much food, it raised my confidence in the trip ahead. Of course, I knew they would provide us with food, but as Ahmed always told me, one should not depend on others completely. I learned this besides him teaching me the life lesson.

"What will you do with the apartment rent?" I asked him, completely packed and ready to leave.

"I will leave him the money I owe him for these few days. It's not completely the end of the month so I will not pay him the entire amount."

I dug the large pocket for my money. Since losing money, I put most of my money inside the large pocket, deep inside.

"No need," Adam said, waving me off. "I am thankful to have

you come along with me. So I will cover this month's rent. Or at least, these last two weeks. Make sure you gave everything. Wait for me outside. I will call the owner and we can leave. It will give us a few minutes to get there."

I nodded and left the apartment. The sun rose quickly, and by ten in the morning; it radiated its heat. I could only imagine how hot it would be out in the desert. I bought high-quality sandals at an expensive price. I had the bucket hat Ahmed gave me, but as I touched it, I doubted it would suffice. What I really needed was a turban; one of those the Saharan wore. Blue and black. Light to wear. They were versatile—covering the tops of heads, faces except for the eyes, and neck areas. I looked around for a shop that sold them. They weren't around. I thought about going to the market, but that might not give us enough time. I kept my eyes open as we headed toward the sand dunes.

At the entrance to the sands, large groups gathered for the caravan trip. I entered the sand, feeling it for the first time. Some people took off their sandals, and others kept them on. I took mine initially to get a feel of the sand on my soles. It was warm, not hot enough to burn my feet, but warm. I imagined it would only get hotter as the day went on. Past the groups and deeper into the desert, there were a few men standing near the camels, some packed with items and others drinking water from large buckets. I could see a handful of men, but possibly more were nearby. Unlike the groups, the men wore the full traditional Sahara outfit—long robes and turbans that covered their entire heads except between their eyebrows down to their chins.

I had bought a long robe a few days since I arrived in Merzouga. I had tucked it inside my bag. And for the turban, Adam and I bought one each from a shop we walked by before we entered the desert.

A few minutes later, one leader near the camels broke off from his pack. He walked to where the groups had gathered, positioning himself in the central area.

"Listen, people who want to risk their lives," the man said. He had a deep voice. "My name is Abu Bakr. If you are here to have fun, if you think crossing the desert will earn you respect, or if you are here for any other lousy reason, I suggest you turn back right now. Your life is at stake here, and one," he raised a finger, "one mistake will cost you your life. Actually, you don't even need to make a mistake. We ask God for help on our journey."

"That's the same caravan leader I met last year," Adam leaned to me and whispered. "After I heard those words, I left. Seems like few people are leaving right now. But I am sure at least half will leave."

"It might take months until we reach the other end," he said. "We are in God's Hands. If it is written that you die in the desert, we will bury you there. If it is written that you will complete the journey, nothing can stand before you. We are in God's Hands. May He make it easy for us. If you are not religious, you will become religious with this journey, during it and possibly after it.

"I suspect a few people will die from the heat, and some might die from snake or scorpion bites—too late for us to rescue them. One or two of you might die from some other reason. You will enter the valley of death. Do not fear it. It never invited you; you invited yourself. Know this and know God. If He decrees that you stay alive, nothing can harm you. In God we put our trust."

I had never been a religious person. I practiced my five daily prayers and sometimes read the holy book. From time to time, I gave a dirham or two to a poor person who asked or fed a stray cat that meowed and followed me. It had become obvious that Abu Bakr had been a very religious person. It made me feel unsure of myself; whether being religious had a part in the journey's success.

A group of three people walked away. They were obviously tourist, white skin and blue eyes. Their departure from the caravan pack opened the door for more people to leave. Most were Moroccans, and not in groups. I exchanged glances with Adam, with both of us sharing unspoken words.

Do we continue onward? I thought.

Abu Bakr continued before any of us broke silence.

"Once you commit to the desert, there is no return option. You commit fully and completely. You put your life in God's hands. Only He can get you across the Sahara desert safely. My leaders and I are only a cause." Abu Bakr paused briefly. He looked at the people who were leaving and the people who stayed. When the people separated, he nodded to himself and address the remaining crowd, about less than half of what originally stood waiting minutes ago. "Good. Now the lot of you, whoever remains, you will need the proper gear. I see some of you have prepared well, and others have not. You will need a headscarf, good sandals, robes, and possibly a blanket—though we have a few that you all can share.

"The payment you give us will pay for your meals during the trip and other costs such as our nights at the oasis. We will rest at a few. It will provide us time to rest and clean ourselves and rest the camels and stock more drinking water and food. Now, before I continue onward with the journey details, I want you all to buy these items from the nearby shop and return within the next half hour."

The word oasis reminded me of water, and that led my thoughts to the dripping sound of water from my dream. The water stream coming down behind my parents. It happened in past dreams, and in the older dreams, I only heard the dripping sound. In addition, in the later dreams I heard a splashing of water, as if someone tapped on the surface. But I could not see it; it happened behind me, just like the dripping of water.

Adam and I walked to Abu Bakr and asked him to help us wear the turbans.

"How old are you?"

"Twenty," I told him, but left out the fact that I had just turned twenty a few days ago.

"I'm twenty-one," Adam said, standing tall. He wasn't much taller than me, but he wanted to make himself seem talk and older.

I had a closer look at Abu Bakr now that I stood less than a meter away. He started with Adam's turban. I gazed at his face. He had a scar on his face, a medium-sized cut that crossed the edge of his left eye.

"You two are sure you want to cross the Sahara Desert?" Abu Bakr moved onto my turban. I looked at Adam's and loved it. It suited him well. "It will not be easy; the Sahara Desert is a harsh environment. And once you're inside, there is no going back."

Those words returned doubt into my mind. I could not think about the troubles of the desert. I knew that once I made the commitment, I would not look back. To counter the doubt, I thought about something else. I thought about the dripping water from the dream, my parents with their hands tied, the crowds of people holding filled sacks, and the pyramids. I brought forward Mohamed's words, and Brahim's. They gave me encouraging words that, when I thought repeated them in my mind, left no room for doubt and fear.

I nodded to Abu Bakr and felt the turban on my head. Almost instantly, I felt the coolness it brought. No doubt, it had been better than a hat.

When everyone regathered, Abu Bakr and his leaders shared more details about the journey—how we'd travel in groups, each group would have two camels, and that each few groups would have a leader. He explained the trip and then went on that all those details were subject to change.

"The desert has no plans," Abu Bakr said firmly. "It has its own schedule, and it is subject to change at its own will. We are the tourists and it is the local. May God be with us. One of our leaders," he turned to a young man, about six or seven years older than I, "Yousef will come around collecting your payments for the camels. Be patient as he collects the payments and forms the groups. Remember, each couple, group, and camel will have its own leader, such as myself or Yousef, or another leader."

I hoped Abu Bakr became our leader. From the leaders, he looked the most experienced. Something about him, the way he carried himself radiated a certain respect that other had lacked. I dropped my bag on the sand and searched for my money. I tried concealing it as best as I could as I counted the bills. In the last few weeks, I saved about one thousand and three hundred dirhams. I kept the three hundred dirhams as a safe net, for when I arrived in Egypt. Putting one thousand dirhams for the trip across the desert was well worth it.

When I had asked the people, such as Brahim, they told me there wasn't a fix price. Each time the prices fluctuated, depending on the caravan leaders and the amount of people for each camel. But the base price, the least amount a person could pay was five hundred dirhams.

Like Adam, I sat in the warm sun, waiting for Yousef to come by. I sat quietly, thinking about my dream and the people around. A few weeks ago, I was running around the market as a rug merchant. Despite all that had happened, I had no regrets. Everything that happened was for a reason, and the result mattered more than what I had lost or gone through. If I had not lost my money, I would not have met Adam or Brahim, or learned to manage a shop all on my own. Maktub.

Yousef approached us, looking at us with close eyes. He wore his turban completely, covering everything except his dark brown eyes. Around them, he wore kohl which made him look more sinister. A medium-sized sack strapped around his upper body, with its front against his chest area. Though short, he looked either large or strong, I guessed the latter.

"Only you two in a group?" He asked, both hands on the sack.

"Yes, sir," Adam said, searching his bag for money.

"For a camel loaded with a tent, meals until we arrive across the desert, protect, and care from a doctor if you become ill." He opened zipper. "It will cost five thousand dirhams."

Adam looked at me, and then my small stack of money—the

five two hundred dirham bills. I watched him. In his hand, he had at least a two hundred dirham bill, but from the thickness, I could tell the money was not enough.

"I have five hundred," Adam said, and waited for me.

With those four words, I wanted to laugh out my frustration. I had spent weeks, went through so much trouble, left my home, gave almost everything up to cross the Sahara desert, and now we barely had half the amount we needed. I could not stay in Merzouga longer while people left on the caravans.

"How is that all you have?" I said, frustration visible in my voice. I wanted to snap at him. I barely had half, but at least I saved a lot of money the last few weeks. I even helped him pay half the rent. So really, he should have had at least the same amount that I saved. "I have one thousand dirhams and I have to save at least three hundred when we arrive to the other side."

"It's all I have, five hundred dirhams."

I rolled my eyes and tucked my money inside my bag. We were not going anywhere with that amount. All my troubles ended.

Yousef closed his zipper. "You two are the last, so if you cannot pay for the camel, you have no place within our caravan."

6

I rarely got headaches. But in the situation I was in, a headache was expected. Yousef left us and I placed my head on the backpack. I wanted to cry. Foremost, I was frustrated with myself. I could not blame Adam entirely. If I had half the amount, I would have blamed him. With so many roadblocks, I wanted to leave. I wanted to go back to Marrakech because, even if some miracle happened and we had a camel, I questioned if it would have been the right thing to do. Clearly, the roadblocks were happening for a reason. It made me think that the entire trip was not the right thing to proceed with.

But then I thought of the dream and the young girl's dream.

"I thought you had more," Adam said, sitting beside me. "If I had known, I would have told you otherwise. I would have worked hard to save more money. We paid half the rent each, but until you arrived, I saved no money. I thought you had more money, seeing that you were originally planning this trip without me." We exchanged glances. "I mean, if you were here alone, you would have been not only three thousand and five hundred short but also another five hundred dirhams short."

He was right. Time was against me. For him, he could return to Merzouga and start working the following day at the shop he worked at. But for me, I had to leave. The longer I waited, the more likely whatever trouble my parents were in would occur. I placed my head back on my bag, frustrated with myself.

"Attention everyone," Abu Bakr yelled over the group chattering. "Attention everyone. We will leave shortly. Our leaders will come around to check their groups, give you armbands—you must wear them at all times—and triple-check we are all ready to leave."

I kept my eyes on him, wondering if my saddened expression would change things. Some customers tried using this tactic when buying things, not from our rug shop, but from other shops in the market. They would use their kids as a way for the merchant to accept their lower price. He found my eyes, sitting away from the group, and simply looked at me. I raised my saddened expression, trying to blackmail him emotionally. It did not work. He simply held my gaze for two or three seconds and then looked away.

"Do you want to head back to town?" Adam said, sitting next to me.

I bottled my anger. I wanted to backlash at him, to blame him for us leaving with the caravan. I knew it wasn't his fault, at least not completely. But his words, taking the trip so lightly, as if we had another try in a few months. I did not have a few more months.

The group leaders walked to their respective groups. I turned to where we had come from, away from the desert. No sign of anyone. I thought about what we could do in that moment. Maybe we could work to pay the rest amount, or if we could pay them the rest upon arrival. I doubted they would accept such a proposal, but it was worth asking. If it did not work, I thought they would at least see our strong desire to travel with them. Halfway to standing, Adam placed a hand around my wrist and shook it.

"Look, there is another person! Look, maybe we will go!"

Fueled by excitement, I turned my neck so fast I heard a snap. I placed a hand on it and smiled at the middle-aged man rushing toward us. He was about in his thirties and wore a turban, and had pale skin. No doubt he was a foreigner. Some type of European. His travel bag looked expensive, with multiple straps on the outside and a pair of shoes and sandals hanging from their laces and straps. When he approached up, about ten meters away, he waved and called, "Hey!" He had an accent, somewhere I knew but could not get a grip of it. I looked at Abu Bakr, who met the man near the groups of travelers.

The pale-skinned man caught a breath and then said, "I would like to cross the Sahara desert." The man spoke French. I could understand some French. We had many foreigners visit Marrakech, so I picked up a few words and phrases. Ahmed always encouraged me to learn languages; he told me that languages opened the door to communicating with the world. I thought it funny at the time because all I knew was that it opened the door to communicating with possible foreign customers. But sitting there, watching the man speak with Abu Bakr, made me understand what he was talking about.

"Am I late?" The man said, speaking slowly.

"No," Abu Bakr replied in broken French. "We have two people waiting, too. They need a little more than half the amount. Each camel costs five thousand dirhams. They have—"

"I will pay," he said, looking at us. The man had blue eyes and some facial hair—a small beard and mustache. He curled his lips to form a half smile. "I will pay, and we will go." He pointed across the desert.

Abu Bakr hesitated, looked toward Adam and I, and then he looked at the man. "Yes. If you would like."

As the man searched his backpack for money, he said, "My name is Gustavo. I am French. I will travel across the desert for adventure. I am healthy." But Abu Bakr, and another group leader who came by, did not care about the information. Their necessity was the money.

An hour later, I had a smile on my face. We had a group of three: Adam, Gustavo, and I. Our camel moved beside us as we went deeper into the desert, leaving Merzouga behind us. It turns out Gustavo knew a few words in Arabic. He had traveled throughout Morocco for the last few months, finally reaching the desert and leaving Morocco. We introduced each other, and the man, to my first impressions, seemed like a wonderful person. Very talkative, but spoke good things about Moroccans and his experiences during travels. Traveled from France to Spain and then through Morocco with only his travel bag and money. We spoke both Arabic and French; a mixture of the two languages.

Yousef became our leader. Like the other leaders, he managed about three groups. As went left Merzouga behind us, Abu Bakr waved Yousef to him, in the front. Yousef let out a sigh and went up closer to Abu Bakr's group of people. I took a few steps forward, leaving our camel, Adam and Gustavo a couple of meters behind. My curiosity drew me closer to their discussion. As I sat earlier, listening to Abu Bakr share details abut the trip, I heard him stop abruptly when one of the other leaders—I think the person second in command—got him to stop talking.

The leaders argued, showing their anger toward one another. It seemed like they disagreed on a matter that made them split into two factions. I wanted to get as close to them as I could, but for me to do so, in order to hear, I would have to leave my group. They had strict rules on staying within our camel's radius. Of course, I did not want to cause trouble on the first day of travel. I observed their heated discussion, somewhat jealous of Abu Bakr's group as they had a direct ear to the leader's discussions. A few minutes later, the groups broke off and went back to their areas.

We walked for a few minutes, rested for a few minutes, and continued walking. In the early evening, we stopped for tea and some biscuits. The tea reminded me of Merzouga, bitter. I heard it had some benefits for a warm body. And then we continued onward, leaving the sunset behind us. Adam and Gustavo spent a while talking since we left Merzouga; they got along very well. I spent a good deal of time listening to my thoughts and planning on what I would do once we arrived in Egypt. But I also knew we had a long way to go before we reached the other side of the Sahara Desert.

"Your friend is very interesting," Gustavo said, tapping my shoulder. "He had an unconventional upbringing than I know and maybe you know."

I looked at Adam. We spent several weeks together, but we still had not talked about our history. I knew he had been in Merzouga for a few months; before that, he had been in Marrakech. But other than that, I had not known his detailed history. We talked about bits here and there, but not about his family or his upbringing.

"Do you mind sharing?" I told him. I had never been someone who continues questioned people about their personal matters. I hated it when people did it to me; I knew multiple people at the market who were nosy.

"I used to have both parents," Adam shared. "My older sister and brother were like my best friends. They always took good care of me, even when they weren't home. My parents were always proud of them. They were top of their class, and they went after careers that had some sort of prestige. I, on the other hand, school was not for me. My parents always told me I was a bad kid because I never tried. I would get in trouble in and out of school."

I had never seen him as a bad kid. At least, in the short time that I had known him, he had never done me wrong, nor had we fought. I had only witnessed good things about him—he invited me to his apartment, told me about the caravans, and taught me things about the locals in Merzouga.

"My parents sent me to work for another family. They told me it had been for the summer, a punishment for not passing that school year. Nope. The agreement was that the new family had adopted me. I had thought all that work in the summer would change my parents' thoughts of me. That I would work hard at my new family and then get paid at the end of the month, and give that money to my parents. Come midsummer, I agreed papers—that I had been adopted."

Adam paused and shook his hand. No tears came out of his eyes. It seemed as though he had already cried out all the tears. I thought I had trouble growing up—not knowing my parents and Ahmed denying me school like the other kids. But Adam's history made me think twice.

"Tell him how you escaped," Gustavo broke the brief silence. "It is very strategic."

"Their daughter helped me escape. She had suspicions about my arrival that summer. The work I had been tasked with was to become a personal assistant to their daughter. She had crutches but could still do most things on her own. My parents painted that story as a way for me not to question my purpose at the new family's home. And her parents shared the same script with me, keeping it a secret for at least that summer, because, according to their daughter, they were not fully on board. At least the two parents. One wanted to adopt, and the other did not. Anyway, their daughter helped me.

"One day, they had friends and family over to celebrate the new home renovations. They all stayed up late at night. As soon as they went to sleep, about four in the morning, I prepared to leave. I left their home around five in the morning. I left Marrakech, and in the next few months to years, made my way to Merzouga."

"It's sad that you had to go through all this," I said. "Being separated from your parents is one thing, but to have your parents plot that separation is another thing."

"Yeah, it is, but since then, I promised myself not to trust anyone. I trust myself and money. All I care about."

I looked him in the eye, and I was glad I did. Because his words, without the context of his eyes, could easily have been overlooked. Gustavo was occupied with a bottle of lotion, so he only had ears for our conversation. Adam's eyes were hard and stern. He meant every word of his last statement. I, of course, did not agree with him. And his stern eyes worried me because they had shown a deeper level of hatred, something I had not seen in him before.

Surely he trusted me, I thought. I definitely trusted him.

7

An hour or so before our first sunset in the desert, we set up camp. The leaders explained the plan in more detail while they raised tents. Some travelers, like Gustavo, helped them. I liked the travel schedule. We'd walk for about two hours before sunrise until midday. Take a break from midday until early evening—when the sun is hottest. And then travel from early evening until a few hours before midnight—when we'd rest for the following day. What worried me about the schedule was the duration it would take to arrive at the other end. It seemed like we'd rest too much. I looked down at my legs; my first day went well, but I doubted my legs would feel as comfortable in the following days, when walking in the desert became consistent and dunes became frequent.

I entered the tent first. For the night, I would share it with Adam and Gustavo. They followed me behind. I found a corner and placed my bag on the thin plastic mat. I thought about my parents while Adam and Gustavo searched their bags. The leaders were outside preparing dinner. Gustavo shared some snacks; I absentmindedly waved his offer. I laid on the mat. I remained to my own thoughts, the dripping water came into mind. The dripping water from the faucet, or a waterfall of sorts. I spun. Only the back of the tent was there. I could smell food entering our tent. My thoughts wandered to other areas: to how they transported meat with such heat of the desert. Each tent had one flashlight, but it was mostly used inside.

The leaders called us an hour later, and we turned the flashlight off and headed out into the dark desert. A cool breeze and a clear sky. I paused to take in the beautiful atmosphere. If nothing came out of this trip—though I still wanted to see my parents, well and alive—it would have been worth it. With mostly darkness surrounding our camp, the sky had hundreds of stars. The sun disappeared below the horizon, and only specks of its light remained near the horizon. I followed Adam and Gustavo, who were wearing sweatshirts. I had forgotten mine inside the tent. We all gathered near a fireplace, with the tents surrounding it. It provided some warmth.

Yousef brought us a plate of food. It had different vegetables, but from what I could see, no meat. Our group, along with the other two groups Yousef managed, came around that large plate of cooked vegetables and ate in silence. After dinner, the leaders entertained us with some of their songs and dancing. Gustavo and some Europeans enjoyed the entertainment, joining them towards the end.

Abu Bakr, at one point, brought the entertainment to a complete halt. "It is time you all got some rest. I do not want to hear complaining tomorrow that you are too tired to walk. We will start an hour before Fajr prayer and will not stop until an hour before Duhr prayer, about half-past eleven.

"Leaders, I will need to speak to you tonight about an important matter. Get the travelers you're responsible for settled down and let us meet at the leader's camp in an hour."

I thought I would sneak out later in the night and hear what they had to say. If they would speak in their camp and they would leave the campfire and torches burning, I could make my way to their camp without them knowing. It benefited having sand under my feet; they would not hear me coming their way.

"Did you see how Abu Bakr responded?" I asked the guys.

Gustavo was still smiling, and I doubted he had heard me

completely.

Adam gave me a skeptical look. "What do you mean?"

"Their meeting is in an hour. It must have some important information they are not telling us."

"I don't think so." Adam gave me half his attention, clearly uninterested. "It's probably just leader stuff; them reviewing our first day and planning for the days to come."

"You saw them disagreeing about something earlier, didn't you? There are some issues they hadn't talked about. I say we sneak out and find out later tonight." I finally got Gustavo's attention and gained more of Adam's. I could not believe my own words because if you had asked me a year ago, I would not have been this type of curious. But the new adventurous me made me want to learn more about our trip and get more involved. The merchant me from years ago never got involved with business that did not directly concern me.

"I am not leaving the tent," Adam said, using his backpack as a pillow. He said those words with sleepy eyes. "Maybe ttomorrow,but I am exhausted right now."

"Do you think they are hiding something from us?" Gustavo asked me.

"Yes," I expressed with enthusiasm, trying to draw more of his interest.

"They will do what is best for us," he said. "I trust them and will follow their lead. If they do not tell us, it is for our own benefit. I am sorry, Darius. But I will stay in the tent unless they call us out to share some news with us. I cannot spy on them."

At the moment he said those words, I felt as though I had been the person doing the wrong thing. I thought about it as I lay on my bag. Was I doing too much to find answers to what they argued for? I closed my eyes for a bit, for that hour. I planned to wake up in an hour to sneak out myself. I overslept, waking up to Yousef's voice.

"Time we leave," he said, his voice inside the tent.

* * *

Gustavo shared his story that first morning, as we walked toward the rising sun in the east.

"My story is not as interesting as Adam's, but I will share it," Gustavo said. "I am from France. Born and raised," he said with clear French speech.

"Oh, really?" Adam said with obvious sarcasm.

"Yes…" Gustavo said. He turned in disbelief. When he met Adam's eyes, it finally registered with him. "Oh, you are joking. I am not good with sarcasm."

I laughed. No matter how much Darija Gustavo spoke, his accent would never have matched that of someone who grew up in Morocco. And the same was for French. I knew French, and many Moroccans spoke it as their second language. But for a pure French person speaking the language, it became obvious.

"So, when I come from a wealthy family," he told me. "My parents bought me anything; the best clothes, food, entertainment, and anything else I wanted. It has been like that since I moved out of my home. I wanted to live in an apartment closer to the center of Paris. I was still being supported by my family, but not as much."

"Clearly money is no problem for you," Adam said, nodding. "That's why you paid for the entire camel all on your own."

"Yes, it is no problem, but I no longer have my parents' money. I had to work for the money. The business my family had got passed down to my siblings, and now we manage it. I help from afar, but they are staying in Paris to do most of the work."

"What do you think is the fastest way to make money?" Adam asked, widening his eyes.

"Huh?"

There was a moment of silence.

"Don't listen to him—" I said.

"Wait, wait, I'm serious," Adam said.

"I don't know," Gustavo said. Thought for a moment; Adam waited eagerly. "Maybe rob a bank?" Gustavo smiled in Adam's direction. I laughed at the response.

"Never mind." Adam sighed.

"What made you travel to Morocco?" I said.

"I wanted to explore, to see more of the world. I have been fortunate with money, so I set out and traveled. I started with Spain and then moved to Morocco. I will travel across the desert, and hopefully continue on way around the Mediterranean Sea until I loop back to France."

"So you're exploring with no real aim?" I thought about the dream. Without that dream, I would not have left Marrakech. I would probably have stayed in that city my whole life, working as a merchant, perfecting my trade. As Ahmed said, I would have gained his shop after him or built up money until I bought my shop. Maybe got married and had kids who will also become merchants. So for me to hear Gustavo had no real aim, it challenged my own beliefs.

"Well, I do not have a physical aim. If you can, maybe my objective is not only to travel without reason. I have a reason for this adventure. I want to find happiness. True happiness. And I strongly believe that it comes from making memories, meeting new people, doing good by people."

Adam furrowed his brow. He looked at me as if I had an answer to his confusion.

"What? Did I say something wrong? I am sorry, my Arabic is not good," Gustavo said, looking my way for an explanation. I had none.

"How can you be looking for happiness?" Adam said with passion. "You already have it! Money is your happiness; it is the universal happiness. Why aren't you happy with that? I would be the happiest man in the world if I had only a fraction of what you had."

"People think money is happiness. It is not. I have a lot of money, but I have always felt a certain emptiness that money could not fill. I want to find happiness in something else, and I hope I can do that by exploring the world and meeting new people."

"I agree with you to an extent," I added to Gustavo's statement. "I knew someone in Marrakech who made money to live day by day. And he was one of the happiest people I knew, if not the happiest."

"You guys don't know true happiness," Adam shrugged.

I found it interesting how Adam thought money equaled happiness. I hoped one day he would realize that wasn't the case. Someone who struggled with money the last few weeks, I understood Adam's perspective to an extent.

"I have it, Adam," Gustavo said. "And if you are right, then why has it not filled the gap of my unhappiness? Because it cannot. Only something else can fill that gap."

When the sun reached the zenith of the sky, we set camp again and rested through the hottest part of the day. I looked forward to the days we'd reach Egypt. It had been less than a day, but I already had a feeling the days would become long and repetitive. I did not look forward to that. Working as a merchant had been repetitive on the surface, but the days were far from relative; days we had bugs, other days we did not, some days we had troublesome burgers, some days we had tourists, other days it rained and only a handful buyers visited. I lay on the plastic mat, thinking about the long, repetitive days ahead.

Near Asr prayer, the leaders called out of our tents. They were all together, with Abu Bakr in front.

"There are sandstorms headed, moving along our path," Abu Bakr said bluntly.

I could hear some people behind me gasp. A man in the back called, "What? Are you serious?"

"How did you not know before we left Merzouga?" Another woman shouted. "I would have left with my sister if I had known."

"Please don't worry. We all know how to get through it, at least for the first one," he said. The rest of the leaders nodded in agreement.

So there is more than one sandstorm, I thought. I did not know what to think. Part of me trusts their leaders would lead us to safety, whether we travel through them or around them. But another part of me agrees with the woman. They should have told us earlier than wait an entire day's travel to share the details. I turned. We covered a lot since yesterday, and though comparatively to the entire journey, we were still near the edge, returning without a proper navigation system was dangerous.

"The first one should be small and will pass by us quickly. The following one will be much larger, but we should be able to make it to an oasis before it arrives," he continued.

"Are sandstorms life-threatening?" One man in the back asked.

"No, they are not," another leader answered. He held a hand on the hilt of his scimitar. "I am a doctor and I can assure you all that you will be safe. But I will stress that we need to reach the oasis before the second sandstorm. We'll have better shelter there."

Abu Bakr continued. "We expect the storm to arrive tomorrow during the day, when we will be inside the tents. We will try to merge all the tents together and bring our belongings inside, leaving only the camels outside. The moment one finishes, we have to rush our way to the oasis. I expect we have time to reach it before the sandstorm reaches us." His voice did not shake.

All I could think about was how this would affect my dream. I had no major changes to the dream, unlike the girl that Bouchra had shared with me. For that reason, I had high hopes.

"That being said, we will pass around eyewear to help keep the sand out of your eyes. We expect heavy winds to pick up by tomorrow. We have provisions if an unexpected strong wind passes by," he said. The other five leaders started handing out eyewear to everyone.

"Since all of you know what is to come, please stay aware and listen to our directions if the sandstorm arrives unexpectedly."

"And don't be afraid to ask questions," Yousef added before

the leaders continued forward.
    We traveled through the night.

8

We spent the next two days getting closer to the oasis. The leaders described the oasis, with many of us, including myself, looking forward to arriving. They said it had palm trees, a large lake in the middle, and cooler weather than in the middle of the desert. The one thing that bothered my thoughts as they explained the oasis was the time we'd stay there. I still had the dream of my parents, and though it did not take a turn like the girl Bouchra had shared about, I still felt the urgency to cross the desert.

I had noticed something from when we set out from Merzouga. The leader's change of attitude. As the days passed, they became more distant from one another and irritable. Their disagreements, at first amongst themselves, became more vocal. An hour before we reached the oasis, I knew the leaders who wanted to stay in the oasis for a period and the ones who argued they had to leave as soon as possible.

One huge dune stood between us and the oasis. We went over it when dawn was breaking. Lush greenery and tall palm trees surrounded the blue water. Many tents were in the region. Cheering broke out from within the caravan. Some groups rushed forward, but the leaders called them back.

We arrived just in time. Dark clouds chased us from behind. They blew sand into the air and had no rain with them.

"Over there—" Abu Bakr turned toward us, walking backward as he pointed ahead, "—is the oasis we will stay. Please be generous and courteous to the people. They are being kind by allowing us to stay with them." The wind picked up, and I wore my glasses.

"Do you think we'll make it before the sandstorm?" Adam asked, looking behind him.

"I hope so, the oasis seems close," I replied, sure that we'd arrive on time. It was only a downhill to the oasis. But the strong wind that followed my words made me second-guess myself.

We walked faster; the wind increased in speed. I was sure that we had the thought of the oasis—it driving us forward.

"We need to move faster," the leader who led navigation said.

I noticed that the leaders had used part of the turban cloth to cover the rest of their faces. I copied them until only my goggle-protected eyes were visible to others. Many other travelers did the same thing.

I turned away from him, determined to move onward. When I looked up, I realized the oasis was closer than I thought, but I still couldn't tell exactly how far it was. I narrowed my eyes, squinting to focus, and noticed a man still beneath one of the palm trees. He used a hand to block the sand from blowing into his face for a moment before running back toward the tents. We had to be closer; with all the sand blowing around, I wouldn't have been able to see him otherwise.

A strong wind caught us off guard. It blew me and Adam to the ground. I laid on the ground and noticed the leaders were having trouble walking. They stopped. I turned around and almost everyone was on the ground. I saw the leaders move the camels in front of us. I tried multiple times to stand but failed until the eighth or ninth try. The wind came from the front, a little towards the right. The leaders had turned the camels in that wind's direction, and the few camels blocked off most of the wind.

"Everyone! Please stay behind the camels," Abu Bakr said in his loudest voice. I could barely hear him. "The wind has increased, but we are almost there."

The entire caravan obeyed Abu Bakr's orders. We found ourselves against the camels, and the leaders kept the camels heading in the correct direction while also blocking as much wind as possible. Two leaders were inspecting everyone, possibly counting heads and ensuring that people were safe.

Within a couple of minutes, we reached a set of palm trees. We still had a few meters to the oasis; visibility had improved beyond the palm trees. A group of four men met us at the palm trees. I looked at them, knowing they were part of the oasis. They wore similar clothing to the leaders and on their sides, they each carried a full-length scimitar. They exchanged brief dialogue with Abu Bakr and another leader. Two of their leaders took our camels in a separate direction while we followed Abu Bakr and the other two men.

"Follow us," Abu Bakr called, waving the caravaners forward. A leader passed us and went to the back.

Abu Bakr and their chief led through the oasis. We walked for a few minutes, passing by a few tents and locals. At one tent, I noticed a woman and a young girl looking my way. They stood near the entrance, covering all of themselves except their eyes. I knew they were women, as that was their practice. Men, though sometimes wearing scarves around their faces, did not stand in a shy manner near the entrance.

I thought I noticed the old lady and the young girl. Though I could only see their eyes and part of their nose and eyebrows, I felt as though I had seen them somewhere. Of course, I could not pinpoint the location. And I honestly doubted that I had seen them. I settled the thought that I had been tired and it started affecting my mind.

We followed a narrow path between small tents. From their size, I guessed each one held a family or two.

In the center, there was a large tent that looked the oldest among them. It had some tears that were taped and had dirt stains on the sides. The chief welcomed us inside. From its outside, it looked large. But when I stepped inside after Gustavo and Adam, I took in its great size. It was huge. Multiple rugs covered the entire area; there were cushions and seatings everywhere, and small tables for seatings. Oil lamps provided all the light inside. On the furthest side, there were seven cushions, large and made with glittering designs. And the temperature inside the tent felt comfortable, more so than outside in the heat. I admired the tent cloth, wondering if we had that sort of fabric in Marrakech, or even in Merzouga when I worked with Ishaq.

The chief and his men waited as we all gathered near the entrance. I stood in front, with Gustavo and Adam at my side. Abu Bakr and the other leaders stood near the chief and his men.

I took off my glasses and undid my face turban. It covered my hair, but without my face. Gustavo and Adam did the same thing. I found the chief's and the people of the oasis's dialect of Arabic interesting. We listened as the chief spoke to us for the first time.

"Welcome everyone. My name is Ali and I am the head chief of this oasis. Six more chiefs run this oasis with me," Ali said, pointing at a few other men behind him. Not all six were there. But the ones who were there looked physically the same, like twins. Ali, among the other chiefs, was noticeably shorter. And one of the other chiefs differed in that he looked much younger than the rest.

"There are many things we do not tolerate here, but one of the biggest ones is theft," he said, and then paused briefly to look everyone in the eye for a split second.

I thought about families sharing one tent. I knew that we'd all have to share a tent, and so theft made sense. I had to make sure I kept my money with me.

"Your hosts will tell you the other rules of the oasis. We need to confiscate all of your weapons until your departure."

Our caravan leaders must have known the rule. They started to remove their scimitars as the chief made the statement. One chief came around and collected the scimitars and took them to a table in the back.

"Anyone else with weapons," the chief searched the caravaners. He waited a few seconds.

"I have one," Gustavo said. He searched his bag, took out a plastic bag, and then took out the small pocketknife inside. It was about the size of my hand. A chief collected the knife and took Gustavo's name, and promised he'd get it back the day we'd leave the oasis.

"Anyone else? If found with a weapon, we will treat you as an enemy," he said and waited a moment or two. Nobody else stepped forward, and he clapped his hands. "Excellent. All that said, Hamza will now show you where you'll be staying."

A young chief, possibly not much older than Adam and me, called the caravaners to him. He left the large tent, and we followed out behind him. We left the tent while our leaders remained behind with the chiefs. Each person carried their belongings. I knew exactly what they were going to do: to split us into groups among the locals of the oasis. I whispered to Adam and Gustavo. We tried to stay as close to one another as possible, hoping to avoid Hamza splitting us.

For a few minutes, Hamza assigned different members of the caravan to temporary host families. Our group became smaller and smaller. For the duration of our stay, we were their guests. The safety of the oasis did not completely cut off the strong sandstorm winds. We continued feeling them, with an occasional gust at times. We were the last three. Part of me felt as though he planned to leave us last. We weren't at the front of the pack, but there were also occasions where he could have set up with a family but chose people behind us instead.

Hamza turned and said, "You three are the last ones."

I nodded. Gustavo said in broken Darija, "Yes, we are the last."

"Follow me back to the chief's tent."

At those words, I grew excited. Were we really going to stay in that large tent? It didn't look like a home, and I doubt any of the chiefs lived there, but I did not dismiss the thought. I wanted to spend our time at the oasis there. When we arrived, the chiefs were still talking with the caravan leaders—exchanging stories and laughter.

"Salam," Hamza greeted them. "Ali, we have no more available tents that can accommodate guests. These three guests are left without a tent." He stepped aside so that Ali could get a glimpse of Gustavo, Adam, and me. "Where should we put them?"

"Do you have room in your tent?" he asked.

Hamza seemed unprepared for the question. His response did not come immediately, and he stubbled to find the right words. "Yeah, I might find some room for three men. Is that what you want to do with them?"

"Yes, find some room in your tent. You can manage three people in there."

Hamza turned around to us and said, "Come on, let's go."

We followed him to his small tent. It wasn't far from the main tent and had very little. A rug covered the sand, and there were a couple of pillows around a table.

"It's not much, but I live alone. You guys won't have to deal with living in a tent with a family; I'm not married yet," he said as Adam and I looked around. We left our bags near the entrance as we didn't know our exact sleeping arrangements.

"What are your names?" He asked us.

"Adam."

"Darius."

"Gustavo."

"Nice to meet you all." He sat on the ground on some thick blankets, near the table. He grabbed a pillow and used it to lean on. "Well, sit down; my tent is your tent."

Hamza seemed like a genuinely nice person. Despite the

different dialect, his voice had been very gentle. We all sat on the thick blankets that surrounded the table and took off our goggles and uncovered our faces, though we kept the turbans on our heads. He did the same, and the first thing I noticed was his sapphire eyes. His goggles had made his eyes look darker. Gustavo and Adam took a seat perpendicular to him, while I sat directly across from him.

"Gustavo, where are you from? I don't recognize your accent," he asked as we got comfortable.

"I am from France," Gustavo told him.

"If I had to guess, I would have said that, but you really speak decent Arabic for a Frenchman."

"Yes, I learn on the way."

"That's very good. I try to learn languages from time to time. It is helpful to know as many as possible." He took his turban off and ran his fingers through his shoulder-length hair. It looked soft as silk. "How about you, Darius, where are you from? Egypt, I assume?"

"No, I am from Morocco, born and raised," I said with a smile. I had a question waiting on my lips, but he spoke before I could continue.

"Really? Darius is an Egyptian name. I thought you were from there."

I had never thought about my name originated from. Now that he mentioned it, I had never met a Moroccan named Darius. But then again, I had traveled little in Morocco. I remained in Marrakech for most of my life, between the market and Ahmed's home. I settled on the one explanation that came to mind: My parents loved that name and didn't care about common names in each country.

"How about you? Were you born in the Sahara Desert?" I asked.

Hamza gave an easy laugh and said, "Oh no. I was like you three a couple of years ago. A traveler trying to cross the harsh desert with a caravan. A Moroccan by origin. I went to Egypt side and then while I was returning to Morocco, I never made it back—instead, I found my home here."

"You moved to live here?" Gustavo asked, intrigued.

"Well, I didn't plan on it. It just sort of… happened. One morning, I left home with the idea that I would never return. I am originally from Tangier, born there. So I got as far away from there as possible, without leaving Morocco. I arrived in Rissani a few days later. I thought taking a caravan would be fun, left with the next one and returned to Morocco."

"How old were you when you left?" I asked.

"I was thirteen. Still a young teenager."

"Thirteen?" Adam emphasized. "That is very young to leave home with nothing. You weren't afraid?"

"I had money. A lot. My parents were rich and worked in the tourism sector. No, not really. I was more afraid of staying with my father than of leaving. I thought staying would destroy my future more than any problems I would run into if I left. It was a risk, obviously. But my mental health was worth more than any money my father and his wife could have given me to stay with them."

Hamza looked down under the small round table. He was thinking about something.

"So how did you end up living here and becoming a chief?" I asked.

"I traveled in a much larger caravan than the one you're in," he explained. "We reached this same oasis coming from the Egypt side—at this moment, I was returning to Morocco. We had planned to stay here for a couple of days to rest before our arrival. A conflict happened, and I became the centerpiece of resolving it."

"Did they ask for your help at random?"

"No, I was lucky to be in the right place at the right time. I'd left my bag in the main tent by accident, and when I went back to get it, I overheard them talking. I asked if I could make a suggestion, and they agreed. Turned out they loved it. I ended up sitting with them for the next couple of days, giving them my thoughts. The night before our caravan planned to depart, they asked me if I wanted to serve as a chief with them."

"Wow, that's amazing," Adam said; I nodded in agreement. "You must make a lot of money as a chief."

"Not really," Hamza said.

It hardly surprised me when Adam's expression turned to disappointment. Each of us had something that kept us going, and for him it was money—but there was no telling where our final destinations would be. There were some things we could do to change our circumstances, but we couldn't change our destiny. If becoming rich wasn't Adam's destiny, then he would never taste a luxurious life. It is something I learned at the market. Old merchants always spoke of it when I asked them for advice. They would tell me never to cheat the customers. That my wealth was predestined. And if I cheated the customers, I would get the predestined wealth and a sin. And if I didn't, I will still get my wealth, through that customer or through other means.

The thought of my parents came into my mind again. I really wanted to see my parents, but I wondered if it would happen. Though I still had the dream, it hadn't been as intense as the times before. I would dream about them once a night. All I wanted was to meet them. I hope the dream would not lead me to some other destiny.

"Do you enjoy it here?" I asked. "Do you ever regret not continuing with the caravan? Your life could have been a lot different if you had returned to Morocco."

He smiled at me. "Yes, my life would have been different. But I had a strong feeling that this was the place for me. That strong feeling is what I hang onto. Whenever I question my life at the oasis, I remember that strong feeling. To this day, I have never questioned my decision to stay at the oasis. I never regretted it and never will… I don't think."

"That is amazing," Gustavo said.

A moment of silence fell in the tent, making way for the howling wind outside.

For the rest of that afternoon and early evening, we rested inside Hamza's tent. Each of took a side of the tent; I slept at the side closest to the tent opening.

"Wake up, Darius," Adam woke me. "Since Hamza is a chief, they invited us to eat dinner with them and the leaders."

I rubbed my eyes and felt refreshed from the sleep. It felt weird waking up in the tent, like waking up in a house for the first time. But considering that I had slept in more places in the last few months than I had in my entire life before, I became accustomed to the feeling.

Adam and I left the tent; Gustavo and Hamza waited outside. The sun appeared and the strong winds seemed to have died a bit while we took our midday nap. More people were outside their tents, about their day. I noticed a few people who came with us on the caravan. It made me wonder how long we'd stay in the oasis. The answer, I knew, came down to the leaders of the caravan.

It was only a short walk to the main tent. A few men waved as a greeting. They sat around a large, round table. A powerful scent of incense filled the tent. It gave me a headache at first, but then I could barely smell it. The headache never left. We squeezed together around the table, clear that the table only had enough spots for the chiefs. Two large dishes sat at the center of the table, filled with vegetables and meat. Pieces of bread were spread around the table too, with empty glass cups.

"Sit and be ready to eat," a bearded chief said, laughing with the others. "We're not entitled to leave anything when we start."

The man was right. The moment we sat with the chief, they stopped talking and ate. A young man came around and filled our cups with buttermilk. It's smell strong, but I loved its taste. It helped mitigate my headache from the incense.

At the end, the bearded chief pulled out a box of dates from under the table. He took two and then passed them around. The chief started talking with the leaders about the storm, the desert, and life far from the desert and within it. I did not talk, but I loved hearing them talk. Adam and Gustavo spoke once or twice, but mostly listened to their discussions. By the end, the box of dates had become an empty box.

The most interesting aspect that I found was that the leaders wore different personalities. Within the caravan, they were very serious and direct. But at the dinner table, among the chiefs, they were laughing and telling jokes.

Later that night, Hamza asked us if we wanted to walk around the oasis and talk, as the winds had settled down. We had no need for the goggles, nor was the wind strong enough to muffle our words. As we left his tent, he asked for our history—where we came from and why we were traveling the desert. One by one, we shared our stories. As Gustavo and Adam shared theirs, I spent more time looking around the oasis. Small torches lit up the area; the fresh air had been pure and nothing like the one in Marrakech. I could hear children playing in the distance. The sun had completely gone below the horizon, but the sky still held pieces of its light. Many tents had only locals, with no caravan travelers.

By the time we had looped around the oasis, we were all laughing and making jokes at one another. It was an evening I could never forget.

"Well, time to sleep," Hamza said. He took off his turban, tied his hair back with a band, and lay down in the same place he had slept earlier. I took off my turban and placed it near my bag.

The next morning, I awoke to someone shouting outside the tent.

"What's happening?" I asked Hamza. He was wearing his turban.

"I'm not sure, they told me we need to report to the main tent promptly," he said with a serious expression. I quickly got up and fumbled through, tying my turban as best I could. Gustavo and Adam were doing the same, looking almost as nervous as Hamza.

The four of us rushed to the large tent. We found the leaders standing together along with the chiefs. Near them were almost everyone from the caravan. Hamza joined the chiefs and leaders while Adam, Gustavo and I stood near the travelers. The chiefs' faces were stern, far from their expressions from yesterday. I noticed a young girl walking near the chiefs and leaders. It was the same girl I had made eye contact with when we had arrived. The old lady entered the tent and took her spot near the young girl.

Ali whispered to Abu Bakr, and then our leader nodded.

"I do not think I made myself clear yesterday," the bearded chief said. "Theft is a serious matter at this oasis. Now we will find the thief, and he or she will face the consequences. Someone from this group has stolen from this old lady and her granddaughter, and we will find out soon who it is. Please point to the person you saw enter your tent last night." He asked the old lady.

The old lady walked near the group of caravan travelers, examining every person carefully. She hesitated near a few people, including Adam. But when she made eye contact with me, she turned to Ali and pointed toward me. "It was he."

9

My heart stopped as if shocked itself. And then it beat faster and faster. She pointed at me as if she knew in her mind that I had stolen something of hers. She made it so believable that I doubted myself. Did I sleepwalk into her tent? I had never walked in my sleep. How could she have been so certain? I could imagine the dark, barely lit paths between the tents. At that moment, I thought she couldn't choose someone, so instead, she selected me at random. It was the only explanation I could think of. And the sudden shock kept me speechless. One leader came near me, and another left with Hamza out of the tent. That one leader pulled me toward the chiefs and other leaders, away from the caravan travelers.

I finally found my voice. "She's lying. She doesn't know. I don't even know her, nor is the tent I slept in last night near her tent. Ask Hamza. Please, I stole nothing.

"Shut up," Ali cut me off. "Your words are useless. We will know for certain if you're a liar or not in a few minutes."

I did not know what would come next. What would happen in a few minutes? The leaders watched me with a sense of disgust. My vision became blurry, and my hands grew clammy. I could feel myself becoming sweaty. I wanted to leave the tent to ask them if we could continue whatever this was outside. I thought about Marrakech, about Ahmed's shop, about the life I had before. Doubts filled my head that all this was a mistake. That I should never have left Ahmed's home. That if my parents were really out there, why was I not living with them? I wanted to beat myself up.

My despair turned into rage. "It was not me! I stole nothing of hers. I am sure that she has nothing worth stealing!" I thought of Hamza; I had to wait for him and try to get him to convince the others. I spent the evening with him. And we all went to sleep about the same time; possibly I fell asleep before they did.

"Did I not tell you we took theft seriously?" Ali's lips curved downward.

I waited for a moment, unsure if I should answer him, but the long silence implied he was waiting for a response. I could feel everyone's eyes on me.

"Yes," I whispered.

"Speak up when I talk to you," he barked. "Did I not tell you we take theft seriously?"

"Yes," I raised my voice, almost shouting at him.

"So why have you stolen from this woman here?" He pointed at her.

"I did not steal from her!" I said, looking at her with disgust.

"Yes, you did. She said It was you."

She could have said it was anyone—but she had no proof. I couldn't believe that he believed her word with no evidence or without me having a say. I wanted to make my case, but I knew it was better to stay quiet. He was taking her side because she lived in the oasis and I was an outsider. He wasn't judging fairly. I turned to Hamza. I wanted to tell him that I spent the evening with him, that he could solve this issue between the old lady and me. According to him, he had the talent to bring justice between us.

"Take him out of my sight. We will have a trial soon, and if we find you guilty, we will let the desert decide your fate."

The man who carried my bag dropped it in front of Ali. I took one final look at my bag, hoping their rules applied to them.

Everything to my name was inside there, including my money.

The two men shoved me outside and dragged me to a palm tree furthest away from the tents, on the edge of the oasis. A man grabbed my arms and held them behind my back. The second man left for a few minutes. The one holding me gave me an evil smirk. I could have twisted out of his grasp—but where could I have gone? The desert surrounded the oasis. And most importantly, it would further show that I was guilty of wrong.

A couple of minutes later, the other man returned with ropes. I looked at them with fear in my eyes. He dropped my goggles on the ground and said, "You will need these."

Ideas of why they needed the ropes flooded my mind. The most fearful idea was that they were going to hang me upside down until I confessed what they thought was the truth. Surely they would not hang me by the neck. Ali had said they would hold a trial for me.

"Sit down," said the man with the smirk.

I obeyed and asked him, "What is your name?"

The two men exchanged looks. He hesitated, and then said, "Mustafa," before they tied me to the palm tree. I watched the desert.

The man who had brought the ropes said, "You will stay here until we're ready for the trial. If you need anything, yell out and hope someone hears you."

I smiled at him sarcastically and then lowered my eyes to the ground. "When will the trial be?"

"No telling. Maybe in a couple of hours, a week, or a month. Depends."

He must have been joking about the month. "What does it depend on?" I asked. He ignored me, and they walked away smiling.

I stared out into the desert. In the distance, strong winds blew gusts of sand up over the dunes. I leaned back, resting my head against the trunk of the tree, and tried to figure out how this could have happened. Was this a setup of sorts? If it was, why me? What had I done to deserve this?

A couple of minutes later, I heard someone approach from behind, but I couldn't turn all the way around to see who it was. When they drew closer, I realized it was Gustavo and Adam.

"Did you take the money?" Adam asked, his expression serious.

I could not believe his words. After all we have been through, he would question that. I mustered all the energy I could. "No, I didn't! I don't even know that woman, and I was with you the whole time."

They sat down on my right side to block the wind from whipping my face.

"They asked everyone to go back to the tents. The chiefs, leaders, and the old woman are the only ones in the main tent."

"I should be in that tent with them," I complained. "She will tell them whatever she wants while I sit here to die at the palm tree." I had to rest after each statement. "Have they said anything about when I will return? I need water."

"No, but I think I heard them tell the leaders it can take from a couple of hours to a month."

I turned my head in a quick motion. "A month?! I thought the guy was joking...."

"Which guy?"

"Mustafa. One man who brought me here."

"But the leaders want this done quickly," Gustavo said. "That is good news for us, including you. They said the storm would settle enough after tonight so we could travel in the morning. They will petition the chiefs for a quick trial."

"Well, I hope so. This sucks." I thought about the lady, still confused how I could have managed inside her tent. I dreamt about my parents' last night, and I was sure I hadn't sleepwalked. "How could the old lady think it was me? Adam, did I ever sleepwalk when I lived at your apartment?"

"Nope, you never did," Adam said, shaking his head.

Gustavo said, "You were with us last night. I could not sleep long after you two. I think Hamza was the last to sleep, too."

"Can one of you fix my turban so it covers my face?" I asked, and Gustavo jumped in to help. "I wonder if they do things to guests all the time. No point in having me out here in the sandstorm. Tie me somewhere inside, away from the gusty winds." They said nothing, so I followed up with a question. "Is Hamza still at the main tent?"

"Yeah, he's helping them figure who did it. He's looking for evidence or witnesses who saw the robbery. Other than that, I don't know - we had to leave before they said anything else," Adam said.

"How about my bag? Were you able to get it back, or is it still there?"

"Still there."

Gustavo, who struggled with the gusty winds, asked, "Do you need anything? We need to go back to Hamza's tent before they notice we're not there."

"Water if you could, but yes, get back there quickly before they accuse you of something stupid."

Adam and Gustavo exchanged glances, and then Gustavo said, "We will get you water now and food later if they do not release you."

"Well, let's hope you don't have to bring me food," I sighed, and they left.

The trial did not happen that day. Adam and Gustavo return later that evening with food and water. They explained the situation, that my trial was scheduled for the next morning. In addition, Hamza promised he'd help my case, considering that I had not stolen from the old lady.

Before sunset, Mustafa returned and undid the ropes. We walked some distance and told me to relieve myself if I needed to. When we returned, he instructed me to sit with my back against the palm tree. And then he tied me again and said he'd return during the night in case I needed to relieve myself again. I slept that night sitting down under the stars.

The next morning, I woke up to Mustafa yelling, "Get up, it's time for your judgment."

I tilted my head up and found his friend untying my ropes. I gave Mustafa my best sarcastic smile and said, "Good morning to you too."

My response enraged him, and he pulled my arms upward, forcing me to stand. His friend tried to take hold of my other arm, but Mustafa said, "I have him. I want you to carry the rope. He won't dare run." His friend obeyed, and Mustafa held my wrist so hard that I could feel the blood flow cut off there.

We walked to the main tent. All the chiefs, except the ones who brought me back, sat towards the back, with the leaders on their right side. The old lady was alone, without the young girl this time. Her back was toward me, facing the chiefs and leaders. They left the pillow next to her empty. The tent had a few lamps for light, but most of the light came from the morning sun. All eyes were on me, except for the old lady.

Mustafa pushed me onto the pillow near the old lady. "Sit here."

I fell to my knees as a result and then took a moment to settle myself. I glanced around, meeting everyone's eyes; they all wanted to play the staring game with me. I smiled internally, but kept my lips from showing it. It was a serious matter, and I had to show for it. The other two chiefs took their seats. Hamza sat on the right side of Ali, who sat in the middle among them. Mustafa and his friend sat on the opposite side of Ali.

"Okay, let's start this," Ali said with a clear voice. It wasn't his angry tone from last night, more so his serious tone. "As the conflict resolver, Hamza will lead this trial."

That was exactly what I wanted. I knew Hamza would be just and fair. Our discussions that first night would help my case. If Mustafa had been the lead in the trail, I felt as though he'd skipped the punishment of the desert and ended my life. And then he would call it mercy of a quick death.

"Thank you, Ali. I would like to begin by mentioning Darius is my guest in the oasis." Hamza gave me a serious expression. Hamza changed his focus to the old lady who had accused me. "This lady right here is one of my people. She has lived here since before I knew this oasis existed. From what I've heard, she has caused no problems in all the time she's been here."

"With that being said, I would like to let everyone know I am not picking sides. The first question is for Aicha."

It was the first time I'd heard her name, and I continued to watch the chiefs, while they watched Aicha.

"When did you first notice you didn't have your money?"

"Well… I noticed I didn't have my money in the morning when I woke up to pray Fajr. I opened my bag to check for an item and noticed my money wasn't there."

"I assume you had checked elsewhere and double-checked your bag and all your other belongings?"

"Young man, I checked and rechecked."

"Okay. For Darius, where were you that night?"

Hamza knew I was with him that night. He wanted everyone to hear it coming from me. "I was with Adam, Gustavo, and you, Hamza. We were walking around the oasis. After our walk, we went back to your tent and went to sleep."

"I can testify to what Darius has said; we were out that night after dinner." Hamza looked at the chiefs and the leaders.

"Was anyone else in the tent with you that night?" Hamza shifted his attention to Aicha.

"No one has lived with me since my husband died. My granddaughter visits me sometimes but does not stay with me overnight."

"How did you know it was Darius who stole your money? How could you have seen him in the dark?"

It took her a moment to answer the question. Hamza brought up a good point—how could she have known it was me? Even the chiefs were curious about how she could identify me accurately. I turned and looked at her, waiting for her to answer, along with everyone else.

"I woke up at night because I heard noises. I saw a man the height of this young man—" She pointed at me. "—running away from my home. I did not see his exact face, but I am sure it was him. The turban was the same color as the one he had on yesterday morning. No one in the camp has a turban of that color."

I looked at my turban and sat on the ground in front of me. She had a point. I realized as I observed everyone's turbans around me. All their turbans were blue, while mine was red with blue stripes at one end. Aicha was smart, or she knew how to speak convincingly, making the story believable by adding one small truth. There was no way Hamza could find a way out of it. I only hoped he had some other critical question.

"Could I go to your tent to check something?" Hamza asked.

"Yes." She stumbled slightly as she climbed to her feet.

"Would any of you like to join me?" Hamza asked the chiefs.

"We're wasting time," Mustafa said. "It's him who stole this poor old lady's money."

Ali ignored him and said, "I will go. Another chief came with us." Mustafa's friend joined them.

The four left the tent, and silence fell as we waited for them to return. Mustafa looked bothered by the long wait, grunting and sighing. The man was clearly an impatient person. He needed to learn the art of patience; he needed to talk with Mohamed—my friend from the market. I sat, distancing my gaze from the leaders and the remaining chiefs.

Almost half an hour passed before Aicha and the chiefs returned to the tent.

I turned and saw Hamza leading them back. He gestured for the old lady to take her seat. In his hand, Hamza held something too small for me to know exactly what it had been. His lips curved into a smile as he took his seat.

"You all must be curious what is in my hand. Well, this will solve the case."

10

I saw the tense in people's eyes as they stared at Hamza's hand. I looked at Aicha, hoping I'd find her feeling nervous. She looked calm, and slightly curious like the others. Her expression confused me, because in one hand, I knew I had been innocent. And on the other hand, I knew that one of us was not innocent. Only one outcome lead to both of us being innocent: Hamza found her money. But that did not align with his fisted hand; he could not have all the money there.

"What I am holding belongs to a chief among us," Hamza said, raising a ring for all to see.

Ali looked at Hamza and whispered, "Are you sure?"

"Yes. With full certainty this ring belongs to Mustafa."

Mustafa raised his eyebrows in shock. Everyone turned to him. He searched his hands and then looked the chiefs looking at him. For half a minute, he remained speechless. Everyone waited for his response.

"I... I heard screaming and went to see what was wrong." Mustafa turned to Hamza with a heavy expression. "Yes, it is my ring. But that does not prove I am the thief. I would never steal anyone's money, never mind an old lady."

"There was no screaming," Hamza said. "When Aicha and I were walking back, I asked her if she called for help and she told me she didn't. Ali and Simo were a witness to this, and you can ask her yourself if you don't believe me."

"I checked inside if the thief was still there," Mustafa said quickly. It seemed like he had responses ready. "That's when my ring fell. At the time, I had my ring in my pocket you see so when I went rushing to check if the thief was still there, it fell."

"That makes no sense. How did you know there was a robbery at Aicha's tent that night, at that time? Were you strolling around the oasis in the middle of the night? Regardless, I asked Aicha something else, and you can ask her if you don't want to hear it from me. She said she never left her tent. She was inside the whole time."

Mustafa looked down at the rug. "But there is one more question you have not asked. Why did she point him out if I had stolen her money? Why did she not point me out instead?"

"I will ask her that question next as of right now—"

"Trade seats with the young man," Ali said with a hard expression and then he turned to me. "Darius, stand. Take his seat for now."

Mustafa and I exchanged seats.

"So it was you all along, and you let Darius suffer?" Ali said. Mustafa didn't say a word. "You shall suffer double now."

"Ali, if I may interrupt, I have one more question for Mustafa," Hamza said. "But before I do, I want to ask Aicha a final question. What made you choose Darius yesterday among the guests? You were quick to choose him."

"His turban," she pointed toward me. "It was the same one that I remember seeing that night. The thief was leaving but I caught a glimpse of the scarf from the back; its color and design. It was that exact one."

Hamza nodded thoughtfully. "So Mustafa, how did you get Darius' scarf?"

All eyes turned to Mustafa. The response was obvious; he stole my scarf that night.

Ali stood with frustrated eyes. "Hand me your scimitar." Mustafa did as he was told with a lowered head. "Your silence says a lot. You entered Hamza's tent that night, stole Darius' headscarf and went to steal from the old lady." Ali took the scimitar and placed is behind his seat. He sat back down, and turned his attention to Hamza. "How did you know something would be in Aicha's tent that would solve this case?"

Everyone except Mustafa turned their attention to Hamza.

"Anyone could have figured it," Hamza said tapping his fingers. "All Aicha had to tell me was that the man ran when she saw him. If he was running away from her tent, it meant he was in a hurry. People in a hurry typically forget things. I wasn't sure we would find anything, but there was no way of finding out for sure unless we looked."

Ali nodded before turning to the former chief. "Mustafa, you have wronged three people in this tent, and so you shall receive three punishments. Since you have stolen and lied to Aicha, we will tie you to a wooden pole in the desert and you will receive no shade or water for two days. If you survive, we will exile you."

Mustafa's expression remained the same, without a sign of surprise.

"For the other two people, they shall decide what they want to do with you," Ali said. "Darius?"

"Yes," I said, confused by the statement.

"How would you like to punish Mustafa for putting you through this trial and stealing your headscarf? Be reasonable."

I have it a long thought. At first, I wanted to give him the same punishment that I got yesterday. Tie him at that palm tree I stay at last night. But then I remembered Ahmed and Bouchra, how they have bought me and taken care of me even though they were not my parents. I thought about Mohamed and Ishaq. I thought about the night I had nothing but a restaurant owner I had never met in my life offered me dinner for free and shelter for that night. And I also thought about the dream. My parents' hands tied with a rope and eyes filled with despair.

"I forgive him," I said simply. I could feel eyes turn toward me. "No need to punish him for what he had done to me."

"Are you sure?" Ali asked.

"Yes."

"Okay. How about you Hamza? He entered your tent in the middle of the night without your permission."

Hamza gave Mustafa a long look, and then turned to Ali. "What Darius said. No punishment from my end. Besides, he will either die soon or face exile."

Ali nodded. "That will be all. We will take Mustafa out to the desert and if you are still alive in two days, we will exile you. Hamza, please go with Simo and retrieve Aicha's money. Look for it inside Mustafa's tent. We will meet you at the entrance of the oasis."

Hamza and Simo left the tent.

"I am sorry that you had to go through that," Ali told me, extending a hand to raise me from the seat. "Is there anything we can do to compensate for your troubles? It must have been tough out there, tied to the palm tree during the end of the storm."

"I am fine," I told him. My eyes gravitated to Mustafa's scimitar. I loved its design and having a weapon of that sorts in the desert sounded like a good idea. I did not need to ask him, as he followed my gaze and then spoke before I shared my thoughts.

"We cannot give you the scimitar," Ali said, looking at the weapon. "But I will talk with the other chiefs. I will let you know before you leave." He turned to Abu Bakr. "You will leave tomorrow?"

"I wish to leave tonight if possible."

"Stay for another night," Ali insisted. "You will be fine. It will be clear weather for the next few days, possibly weeks." He turned to me again and placed his hands on my shoulders. I could feel the strength of his hands. "I would like to offer you a seat on our council. If you decide to stay with us, you will definitely have the scimitar. Guaranteed. But if you do not stay, I will still talk with the other chiefs."

The first thought that came into my mind was my parents. The dream. The whole reason I traveled across the Sahara desert. Automatically, in my head, I said no. There was no way I would live in the desert. Even if I had no dream waiting from me on the opposite side of the desert, I would still not choose to stay behind. I loved the excitement of meeting new people, seeing new faces, and talking to different people.

"I will think about it and let you know," I said, not wanting to refuse immediately. With a quick refuse, he could have interpreted it the wrong way.

Ali and the remaining chief nodded at my response. Aicha and I left the tent.

Gustavo and Adam waited outside the tent.

"So you're safe?" Adam asked as he ran to me.

"Yeah," I said, using the bottom of my scarf to cover my face. "They solved the case. It was Mustafa."

"Who's Mustafa?" Gustavo asked, and I realized I'd never mentioned his name to them.

"He's a chief, or used to be. He helped another chief tie me up yesterday."

"I told you that was the guy they dragged out earlier!" Adam exclaimed, turning to Gustavo.

"Let's go back to Hamza's tent and I will tell you all about it." I looking at the sweat coming down Gustavo's forehead.

As we entered the tent, I remembered they had confiscated my bag. "Were you guys able to get my bag?"

"Yeah, it's here," Adam said, pointing near Hamza's corner of the tent. "He brought it back last night. He said they wanted to check if you had her money, but they found no money inside."

That wasn't right. I had money inside; my money. I walked to my bag, confused as to how they found no money inside. Had Mustafa stolen my money before stealing my scarf that night? I opened the bag and searched through my stuff. And then I remembered I had hidden my money. I placed the book back inside the small pocket.

"They couldn't find my money; I hid it inside the book," I told them with a look of relief.

"Smart," Gustavo said with a smile. We sat down, and I gulped down some water to cool my hot body. I shared everything that had happened that morning, from when Mustafa had dragged me into the tent until I left the tent. There was some bread, olive oil and cold mint tea from breakfast; I ate while I shared with them the details. I also told them about Ali's offer.

"Are you going to accept?" Adam asked.

"Definitely not. You know finding my parents is more important to me than anything else."

"So you rejected it then?"

"Not exactly. I told him I'd let him know before we leave. I didn't want to decide on the spot."

I could see in Adam's eyes that he would have taken the offer.

"I might take it," Gustavo said bluntly. Adam and I turned to him. "If they allow me, of course. At least try it out for a year. You never know. I might stay here forever. But I can stay as a filler until they find someone else. I will teach them some things about money and business. It would help them, I think, even though there is no business here. My expertise in money management might benefit them, but I will definitely ask them. I will have to improve my Arabic."

He had a point; his Arabic had gotten better since I'd first met him. Surely he would improve with time, but it was still hard for me to imagine him as a chief. A Frenchman exploring the world ending up becoming a chief of an oasis in the middle of the Sahara?

"You could ask them tomorrow—they could have you become a temporary chief until they find another person," I said, still trying to imagine him as a chief.

"That is even better for me," Gustavo said excitedly. "I can continue on my journey when they no longer need me as a chief."

"So, does that mean he will take Mustafa's tent?" Adam asked, intrigued by this new idea.

"I think so, but he mentioned nothing about it to me," I said. I thought for a moment. "It would make sense, though. The tent would be empty, and the new chief would require a place of his own."

"We will have to wait till tomorrow morning to find out," Gustavo leaned on a pillow.

"We'll find out tomorrow," I said, yawning. "As of right now, I will need rest. I barely slept last night."

As soon as I fixed my pillow and settled my head on it, I fell asleep. It was the first night that I had not had the dream of my parents in a long time. I either forgot that I dreamt of them, or I truly did not dream about them. I woke up without thinking of them. At first, I thought little of it. I thought maybe they didn't appear in my dreams because of my fatigue. But that was not true. In the last few months, I have been exhausted, but I still had the dream of them.

I woke up worried. I stared blankly at Gustavo and Adam. Their lips moved but my ears did not register what they were saying. Adam tapped on the table and that brought me back into the present.

"You slept all day," Adam said. "We left you some lunch." He eyed the large plate on the table. On one side, they left me some potato, sauce, and some sort of meat.

"What time is it?" I asked.

"About an hour before sunset," Hamza told me. I raised my head and found him across the table. "Let's all go out and watch the first sunset after the sandstorm. It's one of my favorite things to do when I'm not busy."

"Okay, let me eat quickly and we can go." I lifted myself and ate the rest of what was on the plate. Adam and Gustavo continued their conversation about Moroccan soccer teams. Hamza sat in silence, smiling at their debate.

Once I finished, we left the oasis. Hamza took us to a dune on the other side of the oasis, which was smaller compared to others near us. Gustavo asked Hamza how life was in the desert. He gave us an in-depth answer that took him the whole time we were walking to explain. He didn't finish until we reached the top of the dune. It was nice hearing about his daily life, but I was more preoccupied with how beautiful the sunset was. The sun glimmered on the orange sand, and there wasn't a cloud in sight. The bright yellow of the sun transitioned to burnt orange, complementing the sand of the desert.

As we reached the top of the dune, I noticed a couple of people watching the sunset. It was so beautiful that the locals who saw it most of the year returned to appreciate it.

The next morning, we woke up before the sun rose in the sky. It had been a couple of days since I'd woken up this early. Hamza had breakfast prepared for us. He was reading something when I got up. We ate in silence, knowing that in a few hours we'd leave the oasis and possibly never see each other again. I had something else occupying my mind. For the second time, I slept without dreaming of my parents. It worried me. It made me wonder if something had happened to them, or if all that I had gone through was for nothing.

After waiting, we packed our things, and I double- and triple-checked my backpack. As soon as we stepped outside, I noticed the oasis had a different feel to it. There were more people outside than in the past few days, getting a head start on their day. Kids were running around, and men were conversing with each other. Some people were walking with bottles and buckets. I assumed they were gathering water for the day from the well.

"Do you have anyone from the oasis to say goodbye to?" Hamza asked. We shook our heads.

"All right, we should go to the front of the oasis to meet with everyone else."

We walked by Aicha's tent. She was standing in front talking to the same young girl she'd been with the day they accused me. Aicha handed her a large jug, and she walked past a couple of people heading for the well.

Aicha smiled when her eyes met mine, and I reciprocated. We held eye contact until she was about a meter from me. "I'm sorry I had to put you through that. I saw the color of your headscarf and no one had that color in the oasis."

We stopped, and I told her, "It's fine. At least they found me not guilty."

"Yes, well, good luck. Safe travels," she said and wrapped me in her arms.

"Thank you," I told her, gently embracing her. I hadn't expected her to hug me, but it was nice. It showed there was no ill will between us.

I looked back at the guys and then walked ahead. Only half of the people from our caravan were waiting. Abu Bakr was the only leader there, standing with the chiefs—the others had to be elsewhere. I spotted Ali and went over to him immediately. He stepped away from the people he was talking to as I approached, and he smiled. It was strange—I had gotten so used to him frowning that he almost looked like a different person with a smile.

"So, have you made your decision?"

"Yes, I would like to continue to Egypt," I said. "I have some things I need to get done and I won't feel complete if I don't get there." I thought about the dream that I no longer dreamt of.

"I understand," he said without sounding disappointed. "You don't want to feel trapped in one area. But now I need to find someone else to fill in the position, at least for now. I have a few people in mind, but they are like family and… well, like they say. It's not the best thing to include family in a business. And in a way, us chiefs run the oasis so I have to be strict with them. It is best to have an outsider; that is what I like to choose. As I have done with Hamza a few years ago."

"If you need someone temporarily, I have two friends who

might want to fill in that position, at least temporarily."

"Yes, temporary would be great. I will ask Abu Bakr to bring me a Moroccan or Egyptian who'd be interest during the next caravan trip. So if you know someone who can fill the position temporary, that would be great."

Gustavo had eyes on us from a distance away. I waved to him over. He came with a smile. "My friend is from France. His Arabic is good but not perfect. He will accept a temporary role as chief."

Ali and Gustavo shook hands.

"Ah, a firm handshake," Ali said. "I like that. How good is your Arabic?"

"I improve my Arabic day by day. I will work hard to improve my Arabic."

"Great," Ali nodded with one side of his lip raised. "I like a man who likes improvement. I will talk with the other chiefs and see what they say. But we will most likely accept. You are an outsider, so that helps. And you agree that this might not become a permanent role for you. But if we can't find another within two years, you can become permanent."

"That's good. Being a temporary chief is what I wanted."

"I will go talk to the other chiefs right now and let you know."

Gustavo and I walked back to where Adam was standing. Hamza must have gone to get the camels. The oasis had a designated spot for them there, and I hadn't seen them since the day we arrived.

"Did you ask him?" Adam asked, intrigued.

"Yes, but he still has to double check with the other chiefs." Gustavo said, with a wide smile.

"I guess this is when we say our goodbyes," Adam said.

"Not now. He needs to talk to other chiefs." Gustavo said, trying to restrain his happiness.

I could see it in his eyes that he knew he'd get it. "You're definitely getting it. Ali sounded desperate to get a temporary chief yesterday. And having you, an outsider of the oasis, has some benefit that he had not told us about. But clearly, there is a benefit of having you over someone who lives in the oasis."

A half an hour later, Ali came with Abu Bakr.

"You will be the new temporary chief," Ali said, looking at Gustavo. "We'll provide you with Mustafa's old tent, scimitar, and some other things I'll tell you about in more detail. Will you be able to stay for at least six months?"

Gustavo nodded. "Yes, that will be great. Once you have a permanent chief, I can go along with a caravan."

"I have a caravan trip twice a year, sometimes thrice," Abu Bakr said. "So when we are returning to Morocco or during our next trip to Egypt, you can come along with us."

Ali nodded. "Say goodbye to your friends. Hamza will come by shortly and will show you around and get you sorted out." He turned to me. "Again, my apologies for what you went through. I wish you the best."

I shook his hand and said, "Thank you."

Abu Bakr said goodbye to Gustavo. "It was a pleasure serving as your leader during this expedition. Good luck. I will see you in a few months."

"Thank you," Gustavo said.

Abu Bakr looked at Adam and me. "Say your goodbyes. We will leave soon."

As Ali and Abu Bakr left, Hamza came by.

I said goodbye first. "Thank you for paying for the camel, Gustavo. Without you, we wouldn't have made it here. And thank you, Hamza, for working on my case and finding the thief." Without him, I most likely would have been out in the desert tied to a pole, if I hadn't died already from yesterday's intense heat. "I am so thankful to have met both of you. May our paths cross again." I waved goodbye, and then Adam and I walked to our camel. We checked our belongings and packed them onto the camels.

"Make sure you have everything," Abu Bakr announced in a loud voice. "We will leave in five minutes."

As the camels moved forward, I turned one more time and saw Gustavo standing beside Hamza and the other chiefs. I waved with a wide smile.

11

For the next few weeks, our caravan followed the morning sunrise and distanced from the night sunset. We walked ahead, not knowing our exact location in the Sahara Desert. Abu Bakr or another leader occasionally gave us a rough estimate of how many days were left, but it seemed like even they couldn't tell us the exact date of arrival or location.

Some people enjoyed the desert; the weeks spent on the sand. But others grew bored and wanted to reach the end as soon as possible. For me, I neither wanted to reach Egypt quickly nor did I fully enjoy my days after our stay at the oasis. I had not dreamt of my parents, and that kept me thinking all day. I stopped talking to Adam and Yousef as much as I used to. Because of that, Adam made new friends among other groups. Doubt slipped into my mind, not knowing if the dream that brought me here had any meaning.

Most days, when we made camp hours after sunrise, I entered our tent and thought about the dream. I hoped that if I held the dream in my mind right before falling asleep, I would dream of it again. But it never came. I dreamt of anything but my parents, but mostly I had no dreams. The times Adam went to a different group, I pulled the paper with the dream's notes. I had drawn a sketch of my parents' faces in fear that I would soon forget that image: them tied on their knees, their down-turned faces looking at me. If the dream would not return, the last thing I wanted was to forget that image.

People became more on edge as we got closer to the Egyptian side of the desert. The leaders break arguments and fights well, moving group members with others. When Abu Bakr got involved in a disagreement among travelers, people really feared him. All he had to say was, "If you do not leave the argument, we will leave you here stranded." Once he said those words, Mustafa from the oasis came to mind. Yousef and Abu Bakr had shared his story to all the caravan travelers. Whenever Abu Bakr said those words, I thought about Mustafa, whether he was dead or traversing the desert for another oasis.

One late morning, Abu Bakr stopped the caravan and turned with a smile. He typically stopped us around this time—when the sun's heat noticeably increased. But his smile made that morning's announcement different. He had shown his teeth, yellow and stained. I stood near him, about two meters away.

"Attention everyone," Abu Bakr yelled so that all could hear. "I have good news. We have about a few hours left until we make it to Egypt. We will make camp here until later this evening. Once we have an hour left, we will stop and make camp. In the morning, we'll leave the desert."

Most people cheered and clapped their hands. I had mixed feelings about leaving the desert. On one hand, I wanted to accomplish my goal—happy that we crossed the desert and I arrived at my dream's location. I no longer dreamt of the dream that led me here. Was this all for nothing?

"Why not finish today?" An ill-tempered man challenged. He got into multiple arguments with other members of the caravan. Most arguments in the last week. "You said we have a few more hours left. We can finish today."

Abu Bakr's smile dropped, and his eyebrows curved downward. When he spoke, travelers stopped clapping and cheering. "You want to finish today? Go ahead. As for the rest of us, we have an appointment with the King of Egypt. He has invited us to a dinner feast. It will happen tomorrow. We can finish now and arrive exhausted. Or we can take our rest and arrive tomorrow morning. I seconded the motion. The leaders agreed, and you all will follow if you want to attend the feast at the King's Palace."

A moment of silence followed, and the travelers whispered in agreement with Abu Bakr's words. The man, who stood near his friends, waved a frustrated hand in the air and turned to them.

"You want to leave, go," Abu Bakr said, still looking at the man—at his back now that he had turned. "That goes for anyone. You do not have to stay, not with us right now nor during the feast. We are close to the end, that you can finish on your own. I will suggest you wait until the evening, but if you'd like to risk your life during the day, you go ahead.

"As for the feast, the King welcomes everyone. We will talk more later today when we set up camp for the night. I think most of you will love the feast and the day we'll spend at the palace. He is very generous to offer us this, to all caravans who cross the Sahara desert."

With that, Abu Bakr and the other leaders prepared the tents for that day. Adam came back to our camel and waited with me for Yousef to come around. I looked tired, and I felt as though he could see it in my expression. He didn't break silence for a minute until I raised my eyes to meet his.

"We're almost done," Adam said, sitting next to me on the sand. "You look exhausted; we all are. But we made it! I can tell people I crossed the Sahara Desert."

He didn't know the real reason I looked sad, nor the reason for my long silence these past few days. It came from the dream, the lack of it. I didn't want to tell him, as I knew there was no point. I also didn't want to talk about the dream to anyone. I had thought I would become very excited upon arrival. But it meant nothing in that moment. If the dream led me to Egypt for no reason; that my parents were somewhere else, or maybe even dead, then I had nothing to be happy about. If that were the case,

I thought, I should be disappointed for leaving Ahmed and our rug shop.

"I am not going to the feast," I told Adam, poking two fingers into the orange sand. I had nothing to celebrate.

"Are you serious?" Adam said, placing both hands on my knees. He tried to shake me, but I pushed his hands away. "This is a once in a lifetime opportunity to meet a rich man and his inner circle. You can get a job or money. This type of connection can change anyone's life. And you want to decline it?" He gave an expressive sigh and leaned back slightly.

"I will think about it today and will let you know later. My initial thought is that there is no need for me to be at the feast."

Adam shook his head and helped Yousef prepare our tent. I typically helped more than Adam did, but one day I wanted to do nothing but sit and contemplate why the dreams stopped coming to me.

As I lay to rest that afternoon, I could not deny Adam's words. He was right about the feast being a once in a lifetime opportunity. And so I weighed my options. I could accept or refuse the invitation. I really had no reason to refuse the invitation other than my mood not fitting with the feast's atmosphere. The travelers would be happy and the atmosphere positive. I thought my upset mood would ruin their positive atmosphere. I shook my head. No dream meant I had nothing waiting for me in the future.

I decided that I would attend the feast. What else could I do? Arrive in Egypt and do nothing? Like Adam said, the king had connections. Though I had always decided not to, I could share the dream with a palace official and they might help. It was a great idea. I curved my lips into a small smile, for the first time in days.

Multiple vans waited at the end of the desert. I fell on the ground, feeling it for the first time in weeks. It felt nice to walk on concrete. The palace officials separated us into groups. Seven people per van. And then, for the next hour, we headed toward the palace in the air-conditioned vans. Abu Bakr took the front seat of my van and held a long discussion with the driver. It seemed like they knew him very well, a tradition of sorts for him.

I closed my eyes and fell asleep in the moving van. The cool air inside made sleeping more comfortable than outside in the desert. No dream came during that nap, and I had not expected a dream. For the past few weeks, I have slept without dreaming of my parents. So I became accustomed to not expecting it. I woke up to the van stopping and the front doors opening. The driver opened the back door for us. As we stepped out onto the palace's front lawn, I stared at the enormous palace sitting in front of us. It looked as if it had multiple rooms, at least three levels high. The grass in front was green, and I could smell it being freshly mowed. The sunlight glistened at some windows, and most of them were covered with curtains from the inside. We were not the first van to arrive, nor were we the last. The driver brought our bags from the back and placed them together in front of us.

The officials asked for our identification cards, and we provided them with that. I didn't have an official identification card, but I packed with me a copy of a paper that stated my name, age, and that Ahmed and Bouchra are my legal guardians. They proceeded with other security checks, such as searching our bags. It took about half an hour for multiple officials to get through the caravan travelers.

The palace officials provided us with some snacks and drinks. They planned to serve us lunch, but it wasn't the main event. The king had other duties to attend to that day, so they told us he'd join us later for dinner. As for lunch, we visited the dining hall at any time we wanted between noon and three in the afternoon. Even though it was already that time, most of us cleaned ourselves first.

"To everyone who wants to shower," the official said, "there are a few washrooms at the end of this hall. Take turns. Like I said before, the second floor is closed off. No one may take the stairs to the second floor. Like I said, the door behind me is the entrance into the dining hall, and that door," he pointed to a door down the hall, on the opposite side, "is where you can leave your bags during your palace visit."

"Does anyone have questions?" The man smiled at the crowd. He wore a suit and had a neat haircut.

"So we can go around anywhere in the palace until five in the afternoon?" A lady asked from the back. She was a foreigner; somewhere from Europe.

"Yes, that is correct, madam," the man spoke in English. "We will gather in the dining hall and then take you to the throne room to meet the king and have our feast. You are free to roam anywhere inside or outside the palace. You cannot leave the palace, of course, and you cannot go to the second floor. That is all." He looked around at everyone and added, with a smile, "And of course, touch nothing. Most things, hung on the walls or sitting on the ground, are very expensive."

We broke off into smaller groups. Adam and I spent most of the time together. He kept his bag in the small, dark room across from the dining room. After I had seen how many people were leaving their bags there, I decided I would keep my bag with me. It was heavy, but after what happened to me in Morocco, the man who stole all my money, I decided to keep it with me at least until I tired of carrying it around.

When we arrived at the bathrooms for a shower, the lines were long. So we waited and then each took turns cleaning the sand and weeks of sweat. If there was nothing that came out of that day other than the shower, I felt happy. I walked out clean and refreshed. While Adam took his shower, I strolled down the hallway, happy and feeling as if some weight had lifted off my shoulders.

I walked until I came across an official of the palace. They frequently walked through the halls, keeping a close eye on us and there when we needed them. I stopped the man by raising a hand. He looked at me with a smile. I decided that I'd speak with him in Arabic.

"Do you know anything about two people being tied up near the Sahara Desert entrance?" I did not have any plan, nor had I rehearsed the question in my head. It came out awkward and the man's smile dimmed as he placed a finger near his ear. I thought maybe he hadn't heard me well. "I had this repeated dream of two people, a man and a woman—"

"I do not understand your dialect, young man," he said with a smile. "Do you speak English? Do you speak French?" He asked each question in its own language.

I repeated the question in the original Arabic. Bouchra told me this a couple of days before I left Marrakech. "We understand Egyptian Arabic, but they will struggle to understand our Arabic," she had said. It was of no help.

The man shook his head, wearing a small smile. "I am not aware of anything like that," he said. "But there are some who can interpret dreams, or at least they think they do. I do not believe they can interpret dreams, but maybe they can help you?" He came close to me and whispered in my ear; I could smell his sandalwood fragrance. "I do not recommend you visit them, but if you really want to, they can be found in the markets of Cairo."

I nodded and thanked him for the advice and suggestions. Though I agreed with him. I could have gone to someone who interpreted dreams in Morocco, but I always believed they were fake. No one could interpret dreams, or at least, almost all who said they could, had no right to do so.

It was still worth a try. And I planned on asking more officials throughout the day. Adam came out soon after, and then we grabbed a few snacks and sandwiches from the dining room. We ate lunch and explored outside the palace building.

Adam spent most of the time talking while we were roaming the front lawn. I became more and more annoyed by his ideals and way of speech. When I first met him, I thought of him as a merchant like myself, someone who loved the art of selling and had no obsession with money. But since we entered the desert, and particularly since the oasis, his speech has been focused on wanting to become rich and his desire for wealth.

"Imagine if the king adopts me," Adam said, leading the way through a pebbled path. "I will have my security personnel. Whenever I wanted something, I would get it. I will have anything I want; this whole place will be mine." He turned to me. "Not really, but I will have access to everything, and my adopted father will be more powerful than any person I have known."

"And what are the chances of that happening?" I asked, not really bothering for an answer. I had many questions, but I decided never to ask them. His passion for wealth was so strong that I feared we'd fight.

"Well, it is not likely, but I can imagine myself. Look at what happened to Gustavo; he became a chief, a temporary one, but still something more than if he had finished with us and had nothing else to do."

"About that… What are you planning on doing after the feast? Like when the caravan group breaks away." I did not know what I'd do besides ask people in the streets about my dream.

Adam thought for a moment. And then, when he had an answer, he turned and said, "I might explore Egypt for a few days and then wait for the next caravan trip back to Morocco."

I nodded. "We will need money to return. Without Gustavo, we would not have reached here."

"Yes, we will need money… good point."

I still had money, but definitely not enough to travel back to Morocco. It would benefit me for a few days, for food and drink, but soon I would have to find an income source. Suddenly, I felt sad because in a few days, I would have no money, hundreds of kilometers from home, and no dream of my parents. All these last few months have been a waste.

My shoulders hurt from carrying my bag, so Adam and I went back inside to drop my bag off in the small room. There was a bathroom on the way, so I used it. I left my bag outside with Adam and then entered. I looked at myself in the mirror and wanted to cry. I had nothing to continue forward with. No dream, barely any money, and even if I had money, I did not want to travel back through the desert in such a short time. I wanted to return to the market, to sell rugs and to talk with the merchants. I hated myself for leaving everything behind for a dream. Though I respected Mohamed and everyone else who encouraged me to follow the dream, I knew they were wrong; I was wrong in accepting their advice. I wiped my tears and washed my face.

Adam waited for me outside the bathroom. Still feeling the weight of my terrible decision, I carried my backpack on one shoulder and continued to the small room. A man waited near the door.

"Do you want to drop off your bag?" he asked, looking my way. And then turned to Adam and said, "Or do you want to collect your bag?"

"Dropping off my bag," I said, taking it off my shoulder and placing it near his feet.

From his pocket, he took out two pieces of paper. "Keep this note with you; it says the number of your bag. And I will tag this bag with this other note, same number." He showed me the two notes and handed one over while placing the other on top. "It will be safe here. You can come and pick it up anytime. You will find me or another person standing by the door."

I nodded. Them standing near the door was a great idea. There was no way of someone stealing my money or anything inside my bag. If I had known that earlier, I would have left it with them.

"Thank you for keeping our stuff safe," I said with a smile. He tilted his head downward slightly.

* * *

At dinner, the King, his wife, and their daughter greeted us. The king approached all the men and shook their hands, including mine. He had a very firm handshake. His wife went to the women of the caravan, which was only about three, and talked with them as best she could. They were foreigners.

When the king went back to the large table, looking out at our tables, Adam came close and whispered. "Imagine being married to their daughter, Sofia. I would become automatically rich. I would have status and I would have power. But I guess we were born into different families than they were." He looked forward, and I looked at him with a heavy stare. But within his eyes, I saw something different. A deep sense of hurt or terrible memories that he had recollected.

I did not respond to his comment. I peeked over at Sofia out of the corner of my eye. Not only did she have a wealthy family, but she was beautiful. She was about our age, too. Dinner within minutes of us taking our seats. Servers came from a back door behind the king's table. One after another, they came pushing carts of plates. They served us first, filling our tables so much that I had to hold my empty glass. A server saw this and then adjusted some tables, putting some on top of others, so that I had some room to place my cup.

There were foods of all types, meats of all kinds, and some dishes I had never tried in my life. A few servers went around and explained the meals in front of us. Other servers started filling food on the king's table. I thought in my mind that surely we could not eat all that food. Some higher officials joined the king's table; they wore suits and ties, unlike the ones who welcomed us earlier.

With the food on the tables, the king began our dinner. His table wasn't far from ours, so he'd occasionally talk with the leaders of the caravan or a traveler. He was particularly interested in foreigners, occasionally speaking with them in their own languages. It seemed like he didn't know the languages well, but he knew some of each language, enough to have a brief conversation.

I became full, and there was still so much food near my end of the table. I imagined all the food could feed the entire market. Mohamed would have definitely made a comment about excessive food if he were there. I smiled at the thought of Mohamed.

For an hour and a half, we enjoyed the king's company and the food. The servers occasionally came around to collect empty plates and replaced them with desserts. By the second hour, a man entered from the main dining hall. No one has come through that door since we entered over two hours ago. I followed him with my eyes until he reached the king's table. He stood behind him and whispered something in his ear. I noticed the king's expression flip; his expression darkened and the creases above his eye ridge became prominent.

The king sent the man to the door and then stood from his seat. He told his wife and daughter to stay seated; they were also about to stand. Almost all the caravan travelers, including the leaders, turned their attention to him as he approached our tables. Some leaders exchanged worried glances.

"I invited you all to a dinner feast out of my kindness," he said. "I did not have to do this. And now I am told one of you stole a small golden item that is worth a lot of money. A statue that has been passed down in my family for hundreds of years. Now, out of the kindness of my family, as they are with me here tonight, I will give the thief a chance to return the golden statue. You will not face as much punishment as you would if you do not tell the truth now."

No one said a word.

"Fine," the king's voice took a harsh turn. And then he yelled, "Bring in their bags!"

The officials came in one after another, carrying two bags per person. They settled themselves about halfway from the door to the king. The king walked to them and then asked again for the thief to reveal himself or herself. No one said a word.

I looked around at the people with whom I had traveled for the last few weeks. From what I knew about them, I would have guessed no one was a thief. Most of them were foreigners and feared punishment in a country that was not their own. And stealing a golden statue, even a small one, was not a smart idea. I thought that maybe the king, or the officials, had made a mistake. That maybe they hid the small golden item somewhere and that no one had stolen it.

"Search the bags," the king directed the official near him. He turned to the travelers. "Does anyone have an idea where the golden item, speak now and you will be rewarded with half its value."

Adam stood and said, "I saw it in that bag."

I turned to him in shock that not only he stood but also that he pointed at my bag. The official followed where Adam was pointing and then picked my bag. I tucked my hand into my pocket, feeling the paper with the number matching the bag he had picked up. All I could think about was that someone had set me up if the small item was in fact inside there. An official, possibly the same one who'd taken my bag.

The official opened the bag and turned it in the king's direction. He then walked to it and took out the small golden piece of a pyramid and a well.

"Whose bag does this belong to?" The king asked, raising it high.

12

I was astounded. The officer's words rang in my ears, and a wave of emotions overtook me. Mostly confusion than anything. I had so many questions. What did they mean? Have they found it? How had it gotten inside my bag? I didn't know what it looked like.

I was lost for words until another official came from behind me and grabbed me by my arms, holding them behind my back. The first man held my bag and a small item, and they dragged me to the front.

I didn't find my words until we were in front of the king. "It wasn't me, King Hamid. I didn't know it was in my—"

"Don't say a word," the King said with a thundering voice. "It's clear that you stole it. Take him out of my sight and lock him away."

"What? No. Please listen. Someone put it in my bag. It—"

"Take him out of here."

The officials confiscated my bag, filled with everything I owned. I made eye contact with Adam as they turned me around, and he just looked at me blankly. I didn't know if he put the statue in my bag or he saw someone else put it in there. Why didn't he tell me he knew it was in my bag? He watched me, his face expressionless. Had he betrayed me?

I heard the king call up someone as I was being dragged out

the door. "Come here, boy."

It was most likely Adam. Had Adam set me up so he could get the reward? After all we had been through, I couldn't believe he would do such a thing. I knew he would start drooling over money if given the chance, but I refused to believe he would do this to me.

It was a brief ride to prison. After they told the guards why I was there, they pushed me down a spiral staircase that led to the basement. The ground was all dirt, and there was a terrible smell from the sewer. It seemed as if a sewer pipe had exploded nearby. There were steel bars stuck deep inside the dirt to separate the outside and other cells. There were six cells; three on each side of a narrow pathway, and two prisoners in each cell. The guards shoved me inside the one closest to the stairs.

The cell had a small bed on the floor and a toilet. I was so exhausted and mentally drained from the day that I just lay flat on my stomach on the bed, my face pressed into the pillow. Depression swept over me, and for the first time, I regretted not staying with Ahmed and Fatima at home. I wish I were back with them, back where things were normal and great. Back to where I worked, and everyone knew I wasn't a liar or a thief.

I didn't know how I would ever get out of this. How could I prove my innocence? Hamza wasn't here to help me, not this time. No one else could prove it, and the king was sure never to believe me. I could swear on anything I liked, but they had found the statue inside my bag—no one would ever believe me.

My mind was racing, thoughts swirling round and round, but somehow my eyes closed and my breathing slowed.

Once again, the same dream found me. But it wasn't like the last one, or even the original dream. This time, a woman stood in front of me, holding hands with two children—a boy and a girl. I couldn't see either of their faces.

"It wasn't me. It wasn't me!"

I picked my head up, startled into wakefulness, and turned to see what was happening without getting up. Two guards brought in another man; he was short, with dark hair and a cropped beard. The guards didn't care what he had to say and shoved him inside the only jail cell near mine. They locked him inside and went back upstairs.

I checked my watch to see it was a couple of minutes before noon. I turned over and lay on my back, looking up at the ceiling.

"Are you going to eat?" The man asked me, looking over at my cell door. Confused, I stood up and saw what he was talking about. There was a tray with some food; it must have been for breakfast. Well, at least they fed us in here—things could have been much worse. I picked up the tray and took it back to my bed. There was yogurt, which I passed to the man through the opening between the cell walls, and he took gratefully.

"Thank you. Did they give you a spoon with it?" He peeked through the cell at my tray.

"No, they didn't," I replied.

He opened the yogurt and whispered, "How are we supposed to eat it without a spoon?"

I said nothing, assuming he was talking to himself. Instead, I cut open the piece of bread and used my fingers to spread the bit of butter on it. It was obvious why they didn't include a butter knife on the tray. There was a cup of juice. It tasted better than I had expected.

I sat on the bed eating while he tried to eat the yogurt using his fingers. I placed the empty tray and cup back next to my cell door and returned to my bed. I wish I had my books to read.

"So why are you locked in here for? You seem too genuine a person to be in here." The man asked me.

I didn't want to talk to anyone, but since I was dying from boredom, I decided that I might as well since I had nowhere to go. I rolled over onto my side to face him and started to explain how I had ended up here. He didn't move from his seat near the bars that separated our cells.

"I'm in here because someone set me up. They stole an item,

stuck it inside my bag, and picked up the blame for it." I didn't want to give him any more detail since I didn't know who he was.

"You must have stolen it from someone powerful to get imprisoned for theft." The man said. He was intelligent; I hadn't been expecting a wise answer from a prisoner like him. If our positions were reversed, I wouldn't have thought like him.

"Yes, you could say that—but I didn't steal it. How about you? What are you in here for?" I asked.

He hesitated to respond. "I hit a couple of guards at the market. I got angry and lost my temper. I should be out in a week or two."

"How do you know you'll be out in a week or two?"

"They tell you before they bring you down here. Plus, this isn't my first time."

"No one told me how long I'll be here," I told him, growing worried. I sat on the bed, pressing back against the wall.

He looked worried, too. "Oh, I don't know why they haven't told you. Maybe they don't know yet. That's probably what it is."

There was silence. I looked down at the dirt ground.

"Oh my. Excuse me, I forgot to ask for your name." He giggled. "We're talking here, and I don't know your name. I'm Noah."

I faked a smile. "My name is Darius."

"Oh, what a nice name! "I had an uncle named Darius, but he passed away. His name lives on, as my brother named his son after him."

I nodded and said nothing else.

Later that afternoon, a guard came down to collect the trays. As he walked back to my cell, I noticed he had dropped something right next to my cell door. I couldn't see what it was until I moved a little closer to the cell bars—it was a stack of money.

I squeezed my arm through the bars, looking at the money in

disbelief. Instinctively, I called out to the guard, "Hey, you dropped something."

I watched the stairs, waiting for him to come back down. A couple of moments later, he popped out from the stairs and gave me a dirty look. "What do you want?" he said as soon as he saw me staring at him.

"You dropped this when you passed by my cell," I told him, stretching out my hand between the bars to point to the money.

He looked at the stack of money and then tapped his back pocket before raising his eyes to meet mine with complete disbelief. His eyes were frozen wide, shocked. He slowly approached my cell and took the money. "Thank you?" He said to me, unsure of himself. "Now stick your arm back inside the cell."

I obeyed and went back to bed. I felt Noah's eyes on me—he must have been watching me the whole time. The guard went back up the stairs, and Noah kept looking at me as if I were some alien life form.

"What?" I asked him.

"You know you didn't have to give him the money back?" He said. His facial expression was blank.

"Yeah, I knew that. But it's not good to steal. I wouldn't like it if someone found something of mine and never returned it, despite knowing it belonged to me."

"But..." he looked disappointed. "How much was it, anyway?"

"I'm not sure, but it seemed like a lot. Did you see how shocked he was when I handed it back to him?"

"Yes, I did. If I were in his position, I would be too. Any other prisoner would have taken the money and said nothing. It would be close to impossible for him to find out. They would need to search the whole prison before coming into each cell to check." He explained to me as if he had already done something similar. "All I would have to do was to give each prisoner some money not to talk. There are no cameras down here."

"I guess that's the difference between me and other people. I won't take something if I know who it belongs to."

"Didn't you say you're here for theft?"

"Yes, I am, but I told you, someone set me up and I don't know exactly who, but I have a good guess who it could be."

There was a moment of silence.

"I don't know you that well. I've only known you for a couple of hours, but I don't think you are the thief," he said.

It was good to hear it from him, but he couldn't change anything. Not like the guard, and he could persuade the king. The guard and Noah would be good people to plead my case, but I didn't even know if I would prove my innocence.

I lay back down on my bed, and the dark cloud of depression crept over me once more. It ate me up inside, and never in my life had I thought something invisible and intangible could be so impactful. The only thing I could do was sleep, but it wouldn't come to me.

Later that night, the same guard who dropped his money came down and gave me and the prisoners dinner. He slid the tray under a small opening at the bottom of the door. Jail food was not as bad as I thought it would be. Maybe it was just this place.

"You're sentenced to ten years' imprisonment, starting yesterday." He said. It sounded like it was tough for him to tell me the sentence.

There was silence. I could feel Noah's eyes staring at me, but I didn't look up at him. In ten years, I will be thirty years old. If my parents were out there, I wasn't likely to find them, not unless some miracle happens, and I do end up finding them at an old age.

A dreadful week passed by. The week was like trying to squeeze through bushes of thorns, and it was only the first week. I had so many more stretched out in front of me—too many to count. But despite everything that had happened, I still had a pinch of hope that things would turn out well. That tiny sliver of hope kept me going through every day.

Over the days, I talked to Noah, and we became close friends. I talked to him about how I had come to Egypt and what I used to do back in Morocco. He enjoyed listening to me, though he didn't think I was a merchant. The only thing I didn't tell him about was the dream. He was more interested in my work as a merchant.

The day Noah left jail, I felt another thorn bush prick me. Even though this had been one of the toughest weeks for me, Noah had made it a little better. Now I would have to push through every day with no one to talk to, to help me forget where I was.

"It was nice knowing you. Keep your head up, things will get better soon," he told me as he was about to climb the stairs, escorted by the guard.

"Nice meeting you, Noah," I quickly replied. I knew things would not get better; they would only get worse with every passing day.

The next morning, I woke up feeling a lot happier. I didn't know why or how, but I was. I didn't reject the feeling, either— maybe it would make today better. The guard brought me breakfast as he always did, and I thanked for the first time since I had arrived. He was shocked again. I was sure he thought I was some strange person.

I ate my breakfast contentedly before placing the tray back next to the door for the guard to collect. I heard him coming down the stairs a little before noon, and I didn't move from my bed. But instead of collecting the tray through the gap, he opened the door. I lifted my head off the pillow, and he made eye contact.

"Get up, you're being released."

"I'm being what?" I said, squinting at him.

"Released," he said firmly. I didn't wait a moment longer and picked myself up off the bed. I walked in front of him up the stairs to find an official waiting for me. I knew he was from the palace because of the uniform.

As soon as he saw me, the man said, "The king has ordered your release, but you must come back to the palace to talk about some things and collect your bag."

I had a blank look on my face. The only reasonable answer that crossed my mind was that they had found the real thief. I didn't know how they did it, but I wasn't about to complain.

I nodded in agreement. "Sure."

13

I followed the official out of the door. Rain poured down from the sky above as he led me to a car much smaller than the ones that had taken us to the palace for the dinner. The drive was short, and raindrops hitting the glass windowpanes were the only noise to break the silence.

When we reached the palace, I finally plucked up the courage to ask him the question that had burned inside me since I left the cell.

"Did they find the actual thief?"

He said nothing and just handed me an umbrella from the back seat. I didn't need it; it was only a couple of meters to the door. I continued to stare at his back as he walked in front of me, waiting for a response. I was trying to figure out how they had found the thief—if they had at all. Two tall guards stood in the rain as if it were a sunny day. They opened the door for us, and then he told me. "I'm not sure, but it's not long until you find out." He dropped his umbrella on the ground as soon as we entered.

"Just drop your umbrella anywhere," he said. I placed it against the wall and quickly caught up to him before we walked into the fancy throne room. The king sat in the front, looking disappointed. The official told me to take the only seat which was a couple of meters in front of the king. There were more empty seats beside him, and the official who drove me sat on one of them.

"Hello, Darius. I summoned you here because we have found the culprit, and it is not you," Hamid said.

I knew someone had set me up. I nodded and allowed him to continue.

"I have a lot to tell you, which is why we have given you a seat. I would like to start by apologizing for all you have been through." The soft cushion on the seat was like sitting on sheep's fur. I noticed his chair was twice as large as the regular chairs.

"My daughter, Sofia, asked me to investigate this issue." My heart skipped a beat. Had Sofia spoken on my behalf? Why would she do that? "She did not believe it was you. She told me you had easily handed your bag to the guard. If you had stolen it, you wouldn't have given your bag up. Everything she said made perfect sense." His voice was calm.

"To further investigate, I sent out one of my officials to jail the following day to learn more about you." I don't remember meeting anyone the next morning. Could the guard from the prison have been the spy?

The doors behind the king opened, and there was Noah, walking towards a seat near Hamid.

"Hello, Darius. Sorry, I lied to you." It baffled me so much that he left me speechless. Was this all a setup to find out more about me? Why would they have done that if they had already found out who the thief was? Noah looked different with his hair combed and in his uniform. He was clean-shaven now and dressed well—the ripped jeans and shirt he'd worn in prison had been a part of his cover.

"I sent Noah to the jail you were at," Hamid continued. "I ordered the guard to place him in a cell next to yours so he could talk to you, and I gave him a story to tell you in case you asked him how he got in. He found out a lot about you, and now I know what kind of person you are. That was the best way to go about it. You wouldn't have been yourself if you knew Noah was a spy."

I understood what he meant; I had no reason to behave any differently than normal, especially in prison surrounded by criminals.

"Sir, why would you want to learn more about me if you found the person who stole the statue?" I interrupted him.

He smiled, and wrinkles formed at the corners of his eyes. "I will tell you why later. Let us stay with this issue first, and then we can proceed to the next."

Hamid wanted something from me, or else he wouldn't have sent Noah to spy. What more could he want, though? I hadn't done or said anything wrong, nor had I spoken badly of the king.

Hamid turned around towards the door Noah had come out of and called out, "Bring out the cook."

A tall, slender man walked into the throne room, followed by an official. He wore an apron and didn't make eye contact with anyone, keeping his eyes on the ground. The official grabbed two seats from beside the king and placed them perpendicular to us on my right-hand side. Noah remained seated, and I realized that he was very close to the king or very important. He resembled him a little, but not enough for me to know for sure if they were family. Hamid had a beard that covered half his face, while Noah was cleanly shaven.

"The person who called you out when I offered them money asked me if he could work at the palace. He wanted to work here instead of receiving the reward. I asked him where he would like to work. He told me anywhere, so I gave him a place in the kitchen." I focused intently on Hamid as he spoke. "The night Sofia asked me to look into it, I asked one of my officials to monitor Adam. If anyone knew about the thief, it would be him, as he had known where to find the statue."

"After three days, there was still nothing. I began to believe it was not him, but on the fourth day, we got the evidence we were looking for. He was talking to the cook." Hamid pointed at the cook. I looked at him, and he was still looking at the ground, avoiding all eye contact. "The official next to him heard them talking about how he worked in the kitchen. Adam slipped up and told the cook he was the person who snuck the statue inside your bag."

I knew it was him. He was the only other person who had had access to my bag in the palace, and he had had the opportunity while I used the bathroom. But I still couldn't understand why he chose money over me. I thought we were friends.

"Cook, I will not punish you since the official came to my quarters right away and informed me. There was no way of telling whether you would have told me or not. But I will assume you would have, since you have done nothing wrong in all the time you have worked here. You may get back to work." Hamid said.

The cook got up from his seat, looked at Hamid and lowered his head as a sign of thanks. He retraced his steps back to the door he had entered through.

"Since we have the correct person who stole the statue, you are free. I would like to ask you a favor, though," Hamid said.

Why would the king want a favor from me? But before Hamid could continue, someone opened the main doors of the throne room behind me.

Hamid looked up at them before I turned around to check who it was. "I'll ask you after we finish this. I didn't think they would come by this quickly."

I turned around and saw Adam, held in place by two officials. He looked down, too embarrassed to look at me. After all we'd been through, he had chosen money over me. He didn't even have the decency to look me in the eye.

"I have already given my sentence for what he has done. Now it's your turn, Darius." Hamid said.

It confused me as to what he meant at first, but then I understood. He wanted me to decide a punishment for Adam for putting me through this, just like the chiefs in the desert. I looked up at Adam and waited until his eyes met mine.

"I forgive him for all he has done to me." I looked back at Hamid.

Everyone looked surprised except Hamid, who smiled. "Are you sure?"

"I'm positive," I said firmly.

"Well, that was easy. Take him out of here," Hamid said. The two officials dragged Adam out of the throne room.

"Now for the favor I would like to ask of you," Hamid said. "I will let Noah explain his purpose at the jail."

"I was at the jail to observe you and learn more about you as a person. I found out you are a great person and you don't take what is not yours." Noah blurted. I knew what he meant before he could finish. "The money the guard dropped could have been yours, as could the yogurt you shared with me the first time I met you—and much more."

Noah looked at Hamid for confirmation before he said anything else. Hamid nodded, and Noah continued, "The king would like to ask you to be his—"

"Treasurer," Hamid interrupted.

There was complete silence. It confused me why the king wanted me to become treasurer. Surely there were more qualified people out there who could do it? I certainly wasn't one of them.

Hamid broke the silence. "Noah told me you used to be a merchant and that you are trustworthy. I have my full trust in Noah. He is my closest friend."

"Thank you for the offer, Your Majesty," I said. I had a feeling he would not be happy with what I was about to tell him. "But I have to find my parents as soon as possible." He looked at me intently. "Is there not a more qualified person to be your treasurer?"

The throne room was quiet once again. He lowered his gaze, and I waited for him to respond.

"I wish you would take my offer and become my treasurer for

at least this month. There will be people coming from all over Egypt to collect rice and grain as I give it out annually. If you help me out this month, I will help you find your parents, if they are in Egypt."

I liked the sound of that. I had nothing to go about in finding my parents. It could take me much longer than a month to find them, if I had the ability to do so. It was my best option, but I still hadn't known why me.

"But why do you want me?" I asked again.

"You're trustworthy. You have merchant experience, from what Noah told me. You are young, so if you end up deciding on staying after you find your parents, I would like to have you come back. There is another, bigger reason, but I will not tell you today. It will have to be for another day." Hamid tried to convince me.

I felt like I had to take his offer at that point. There was a bigger reason at play, and I would not find out what it was unless I stayed.

"Okay, I will stay."

The king jumped up out of his seat with excitement, raising his hands into the air in celebration.

"That is great to hear. I have already arranged for your bags to be taken to your new room. Noah will take you there now."

I liked the thought of living in the palace. But all I wanted was to find my parents. All of this would be for nothing if I didn't manage that.

"Follow Noah to your room. You'll be called down for dinner when it is ready." Hamid said, and Noah and I stood up. I followed Noah out the door behind Hamid.

"It's an enormous palace," Noah turned around and told me as he pushed the door open. "Just remember, all the bedrooms are on the second level and everything else is on this level."

Once we got up to the second level, it smelt like lavender and rose petals. He showed me to my room; it was at least six times the size of my room back in Morocco. The bed was twice the size of my old bed and covered with at least half a dozen pillows. A large wardrobe was against the wall between my bed and the windows. There was a small table with two wooden chairs near the window, at least half as tall as me.

"This room is all for me?" I asked Noah in disbelief.

"Yes, all of it." He said as I inspected the room. A large plasma television hung on the wall across from my bed. Near the door, there was a small couch and a sofa chair.

I lost track of how long I had been standing near the door.

"Well, I'll let you settle down. Someone will come by to call you down for dinner."

"Okay great. Thank you." I responded, not giving him my full attention.

It wasn't until Noah left that I noticed my bag on the ground beside my new bed. I approached the bed and ran my hands over the soft sheets before jumping on it. It felt like I would sink into it; I couldn't believe how soft it was. I had thought nothing could be this soft or plush until now. Compared to this, my old bed was a rock.

I lay quietly in the room and gazed at the ceiling. It was still raining outside. It was an unpleasant day, but for me; it was one of the best days I'd had in the past few months. I was no longer stuck in jail for something I hadn't committed. I had a new job and a promise that the king of Egypt would help me locate my parents if they were in fact in the country.

But I couldn't stop thinking of Adam. I had called him my best friend—but he had betrayed me; but he got what he deserved. His love of money had got the best of him—he hadn't even pointed out the statue until the king mentioned the cash reward. His first mistake had been stealing it, and his second had been staying at the palace. If he had taken the money and left, it would have been much harder to find him. I would have spent the next ten years languishing away in a prison cell.

I sat up and crossed my legs. It was no use thinking about him now. It was in the past. I took out a book I had in my bag and settled in to read for a while.

Later that night, a lady knocked at my room and told me dinner was ready. I dropped my book on the bed and followed her to the dining room. She must have been a maid, but she wasn't like any maid I had ever seen before. She dressed in extravagant clothes and took care of herself. The royal family must have paid her lavishly.

She led me to the dining room—it wasn't as large as the great hall or the throne room, but it was much larger than anywhere else I had ever been before. In the middle of the room was a round table, and the royal family and Noah already sat at their seats.

"Salam," I greeted them as I took the empty seat beside Noah. He was talking to Hamid, and Nisrina and Sofia were talking to one another. They returned the greeting and went back to their conversations. I sat there without making a sound, looking at the table. There was still no food yet, but I hoped they would serve us. I was getting hungry.

It felt awkward sitting there until Nisrina asked me, "So what do you study?"

I had dropped out of school, and I didn't want to answer her. Surely she would think I was uneducated. The only thing I could think to say was to explain why I had dropped out.

"I left school at a young age. I had to help the people who raised me," I told her truthfully. Once Ahmed and Fatima took me in, I couldn't tell them I wanted to go to school and not work. I had to work with Ahmed; it was the least I could do since he had brought me up.

"You mean your family?"

"No, I haven't lived with my parents for a long time." Hamid and Noah turned towards me. "I don't know what happened, but I lived with another family for most of my life. I'm an orphan, but I didn't enjoy being called that." The looks on their faces told me they hadn't been expecting that.

"Oh, I'm so sorry to hear that. Did they pass away?" Nisrina asked. I saw Hamid give her a nudge, which I believed was to reprimand her for asking something so personal. "If you don't mind my asking," she added.

"No, I don't think so. I believe they are somewhere in this country."

"That's good. You seem intelligent."

"It's from talking to all the merchants in my hometown," I smiled slightly. "I also read books sometimes; maybe that helps, too."

"Well, if you want to come by tomorrow to the study room, you're welcome to. Unless Hamid needs you for something else," she looked at Hamid, who turned his attention back to Noah.

"It's fine, we'll do business in the afternoon," Hamid told her and went back to his conversation.

"I teach Sophia here myself." She tapped her on her back. "You seem to be around her age." As soon as I looked at her eyes, I suddenly became lost. I tried so hard to avoid making eye contact to prevent that from happening, but sometimes it was unavoidable

"I'm twenty years old," I told Nisrina.

"I'm eighteen years old," Sofia told me with a wide smile on her face. Her voice sounded so soft and gentle, just like her father's.

Not long after, meals flooded the table. The food filled me up long before everyone else finished, so I sat there waiting patiently for the rest of them.

"Eat, Darius, don't be shy," Hamid told me as he pointed with his knife at the food.

"Thank you, but I am full."

Even the juice they served was amazing: freshly squeezed mango, strawberries, and banana—at least, that's what I thought it was. There might have been more fruit that I couldn't recognize or didn't know the name of.

After we had dinner, I walked up to my room with Noah. He also lived there, and I guessed that he must not have had a family if he lived in the king's palace.

"This is my room," he said, holding his door open as he turned to face me. "In the morning someone will come knocking at your door for breakfast. It might be me. We will also have a meeting with your job after lunch. The king has some things he needs to do in the morning."

"Okay, that sounds good. Goodnight."

"Goodnight, Darius." He said, then closed the door behind him.

My room was right beside his, only a couple of steps down the hallway. I entered and flicked on the lights, amazed once more at the luxury. I still couldn't believe it. The television was at least four times the size of Ahmed and Fatima's, and I turned it on. There were buttons on one remote that I couldn't figure out the purpose of, and I set about trying to learn what they all did until I fell asleep.

14

I woke up early the next morning and meditated for the first time since leaving Morocco. The sun shone brightly through the open window, and once I finished my meditation, I looked out at the view. There was a large grass field, I thought must be the back of the palace. I couldn't see any guards outside, but there must have been at least a couple of them hiding; maybe in the bushes around the edge of the field. I couldn't believe there would be none.

Noah came by not too long after I completed my morning routine.

"It's time for breakfast, Darius."

He led the way to the dining room. It must have been the place where the royal family ate their meals when there were no guests. Hamid sat at the table alone, looking through a pile of papers with his glasses sliding down his nose. As we entered, he looked up.

"Noah, can you look at this?"

Noah walked toward the table briskly to look over Hamid's shoulder. I took the same seat as yesterday, near Noah. I was still wondering what the bigger reason Hamid had for asking me to stay was. What was so special about me? I wanted to ask him about it, but he looked busy with the papers.

A couple of minutes later Nisrina and Sofia came into the

room. I turned around and caught Nisrina's gaze. "Are you ready for your first lesson?"

"Yes, ma'am," I replied. I didn't know how to address her, but I wanted to sound respectful because she was the Queen.

She smiled as she pulled her seat out. "Just call me Nisrina."

Breakfast was a lot fancier than I thought it would be. I didn't understand how this family could eat so much! They must have gotten used to eating until they could no longer fit anything in their stomachs.

After we all finished breakfast, Hamid and Noah collected the papers and left the room. I could tell that whatever the papers were for was very stressful for them. I just hoped it wasn't similar to what Hamid wanted me for. The last thing I needed was stress.

"Let's go upstairs to the study room," Nisrina said, and Sofia and I followed her upstairs. The study room was located at the opposite end of the hall from my bedroom. We sat down at a round table, and Nisrina launched into the lesson immediately. She taught us some weird things. I didn't understand in the beginning, but I grew to understand as I followed the lesson. She showed us different methods of how she would usually go about solving a math problem, but they still worked. Sofia was a genius, or she had already learned the material. She solved the problems in less than half the time it took me.

After we went over a couple of math problems, Sofia played the piano with a man who came in to teach her. I didn't play the piano, so I just sat and watched. I didn't know how hard it was, but she looked very talented. She barely looked at her hands as she moved her fingers nimbly over the keys, and her playing sounded beautiful to me.

"How long have you been playing?" I asked Sofia after she had finished.

"Since I was five. My parents wanted me to learn from a young age. I didn't enjoy it at first. I hate it. I grew to love playing, though." She said.

"You're amazing. Do you still need a teacher?" I asked. He was packing his things in the distance. I sat next to Nisrina while Sofia sat on a stool in front of the piano.

Sofia moved closer to us while remaining seated and whispered, "No, not really."

Nisrina turned towards me and said, "We will get rid of him soon. He costs a lot of money."

In my mind, I thought if he was not useful, then they should get rid of him. Use the money to give to the poor who needed it. I remained silent, only reciprocating Sofia's smile.

Before we had lunch, Noah called me to the dining room. Hamid was already seated at the empty table, with more papers.

"Sit down, Darius," he instructed me with a soft smile. I did so, claiming a seat across from him. Noah took the seat next to him.

"So, I need to tell you what your job will be for this month." Hamid sifted through the papers. "It's not much. We used to have a treasurer who told us that there would be a shortage of crops. We've produced a lot of grain and wheat over the past couple of years, but this year there wasn't as much." Hamid paused.

Noah pushed his seat back. "We're handing grain and wheat to people in need. You will assist me every afternoon with it and correctly distributing the right amount to each family."

"So families will come to the palace to pick up their share?" I asked.

"Yes, they will enter the throne room. The king will not be here. Just me, you, and a bunch of guards." Noah answered. It felt like a business meeting. They weren't smiling anymore.

"I have other things I need to attend to, so I will not be here, no. I might show up a couple of days in the month, but this is the busiest time of the year for me." Hamid added.

"So you want me to assist you with the distribution and make sure we distribute the correct amount?" I confirmed.

"Basically."

That couldn't be it. The king must have wanted me to be here for another reason, one he hadn't told me. Anyone could do this job, even his daughter!

"When will you tell me the other reason you require me for?" I asked the king.

"I wish I could tell you, but I can't because if I do, it might ruin everything. I promise to tell you toward the end of the month. Or ask you, since it's more of a question," he said.

Ask me? Did he mean that he would ask me for a favor? Had he given the same offer to Adam before he went to prison? Would he have been in my position?

"Do you have questions you'd like to ask us? We will begin in a couple of days." Noah asked.

"No, I don't have any," I said, faking a smile.

The next couple of days became repetitive. I had lessons with Sofia in the morning, and I usually kicked around the ball in the field behind the palace after lunch. I would study some more before dinner, eat, and then retire to my room. I knew I could get used to this kind of lifestyle, but finding my parents was a lot more important to me. The king started his search, as he had told me, but I heard no more updates than that. I often contemplated whether I had made the right decision in staying.

On my fourth day at the palace, I began my work as treasurer. As I walked to the dining room for breakfast, I noticed several officials hurrying to the throne room. They must have been preparing for the people who would arrive shortly.

The morning was the same as the previous days, with lessons in the library. They dedicated one day of the week to each subject, and that morning was French. Over the past four days, I had learned more about Nisrina than Sofia. Sofia was timid and didn't talk much. Sometimes she would only say a couple of words during the whole lesson. Conversations were mostly between Nisrina and me.

We all gathered around the dining table for lunch, except for

Hamid, who must have been elsewhere.

"Eat up, Darius, you'll need as much energy as you can get for today," Noah told me as servers filled the table. I found it hard to believe that I would need a lot of energy for this job. If it was exactly what they had explained to me, then it shouldn't be too bad. Unless we worked late into the night, in that case, I would get hungry.

"Follow me; we're going to the throne room. Everything should be all set up. Other officials have been setting up everything since the break of dawn." Noah said as he stood up, and I followed him down the busy hall. We entered the throne room and I couldn't believe how many bags of wheat and grain there were. All the items were ready to be distributed, and the bag was the size of a regular-sized car.

"Does each family get a bag?" I asked Noah, "It's too much for a single-family; it could take them at least five years to finish."

Other things distracted him, and it took him a moment to answer me. "They don't take all of it. We split it into smaller bags. Depending on family size and some other things." He pulled a piece of paper out of his pocket.

"Please take a seat here," Noah pointed at a seat near the king's seat. "This paper has all the names of the families who will show up today. Your job is to ask for their name, then tell me how many bags they will get. I will be right back." He dashed off to a group of officials. I sat there quietly, observing everyone. There wasn't much talking compared to earlier in the halls. Everyone was doing his or her job. There were only a handful of officials, as they completed most of the heavy work. Four guards stood near the main door, talking among themselves.

The first family that came in was a man and woman with a young kid, who might have been their son. They wore ragged clothes and their faces screamed starvation. They did not seem like a wealthy family at all.

"Your family name, please," I spoke up as they stood in front of me, loud and clear.

They looked up at me, then the man spoke softly, "Majid."

"The Majid family gets three bags of grain and two bags of rice," I called out to Noah, reading off the paper. The writing was a little different from what I was used to reading. Moroccan Arabic differed from Egyptian, but I understood it and could speak it well enough.

It was a busy day of taking names and reporting amounts. By the end of the day, I guessed that we must have seen a hundred families. But not that taxing, and I still couldn't figure out why the king wanted me to do it.

For the next couple of days, it was the same routine from afternoon to dinnertime. I asked some families to return the next day, as we could not finish seeing all of them in a single day. One day there was a family who argued about their portions and asked for more. I was astonished by how they acted. I thought they should be thankful for what they were given, even if they wanted more. The king was not required to do this; he was doing this out of the kindness of his heart. Noah gave them their portion and asked them nicely to leave, and once the guards took a step forward, they left quickly and quietly.

The following week, I became so used to calling out the names to the point I began to dread it, and spent my time slouched in the chair. I asked for their name; they told me, and I reported to Noah. Repeat. Repeat. Repeat. Noah left sometimes, but Noah didn't allow me to leave unless it was an emergency.

One day, a man and a woman walked into the throne room. They were the last family to pick up their share on that day. The man and woman looked familiar, and I stared into their eyes. I didn't know where I had seen them before. For all I knew, they could have been with me during the trip across the desert. The man was slightly taller than his wife, who attached to his side like a child to their mother.

"What is your surname?" I asked, racking my brains for why I seemed to know their faces.

"Amari," the man whispered.

"You two don't have any children, correct?" I asked.

The lady wept. I immediately felt guilty.

"I'm sorry if I have hurt you. I'm making sure because it says none here. I don't want to give you the wrong amount." I thought they would have at least one child, from how old they looked.

"We don't anymore. We had a son." The man said with a raspy voice. His face crinkled, and he was about to cry.

It felt as though time slowed and the world stopped. I placed my list down on my seat and walked up to them, my gaze locked on both of them. Could it be?

"Why are you looking at me like that?" The lady asked me, sniffing.

I stared at them blankly. I had finally figured out why their faces were so familiar to me. Some of their features had changed since I had last seen them, but I knew their faces and my own. I couldn't believe they were here.

They were my parents.

15

"When did you lose your son?" I asked. I realized immediately that it wasn't a good thing to ask, but it was too late now. "If you don't mind my asking."

I turned around to Noah, who was waiting for me to tell him how many bags the family was getting. "Two bags each for this family. That's what it says on the paper." As soon as I saw Noah, I saw in his eyes that he was confused by what I was doing. He also looked shocked that I asked them something like that, but I couldn't resist. I needed to know.

I turned back to them. "Why do you want to know?" The man asked.

"I've been an orphan since I was six years old," I told them. I could have told them more, but I didn't want to until I was certain. I could sense everyone's eyes on me.

"I don't have my parents. You two don't have your son." I continued. The man and woman exchanged looks as their eyes widened. The woman held the man's arm and did not let go.

"What is your name?" the man asked, his voice sounding raspy.

"The people who picked me up from the orphanage said they kept my name as it was," I said. In my mind, I knew this would prove whether they were my parents. My name is the only thing that has stayed with me since birth. If they were my parents, they would have remembered my name. "My name was, and still is, Darius."

The man rushed up to hug me, and I stumbled backward. I saw the woman fall to the ground, her hands over her face as tears streamed down her cheeks. Their reactions only confirmed it.

I left my father and walked over to Noah. "Could I leave with these two people and be back before dinner?"

Noah looked at my parents and hesitated to give me a response. "Dinner is close, Darius. You can talk to them in the hall. You can visit them tomorrow morning."

I approached my parents, who were staring at me as I turned around. I wasn't able to contain my smile. We had so much to catch up on. I put my arms around each of them. "I'm sorry, but I don't know your names."

"I'm Karim, and this is your mother, Amina," Karim told me. I was taller than both of them. I had so many questions to ask them, but by the time we got to the hall, I didn't know where to start.

"Where have you been all these years?"

"I've lived with another family since they took me out of the orphanage. What are you two doing in Egypt?" I asked.

"You've changed so much," Amina said, drawing me closer for a hug. "We always lived in Egypt. Where were you living?"

"I grew up in Morocco."

They both looked at each other. "How did you get to Morocco?" Karim asked, raising one eyebrow.

"I don't know, someone left me at an orphanage there and adopted me," I told them. I thought about it for a second, and then it came to me. "Whoever stole me from you must have sent me to Morocco… someone stole me from you two, wasn't I?"

Amina looked at me. "Yes. We spent months looking for you, but no one could find you, nor the person who took you away from us." There was a pause, and then Amina continued. "The officials are skeptically looking at us. We'll continue our talk tomorrow morning. Please come by. It's a shame you're not allowed to come to our home tonight."

It was tough to see them go. Even though I saw them, I was not happy to see them go. I wanted to be with them longer. It felt like I was only with them for two seconds. But I felt better now that I had found them. I hugged them; a hug in which I didn't want to let go. "I will be at your front door early tomorrow morning. We can keep talking until lunchtime until I need to go back to the palace." I promised them.

An official escorted me back to the throne room, while another official escorted my parents from the palace. There was so much joy inside me, and it filled my mind with thoughts of my parents.

Noah, Nisrina, and Sofia sat at the dining table when I arrived. Right when I pulled my chair to sit down, Noah asked. "So those are your parents?"

I paused for a moment. "Yes, they are." I looked at him with the same unrestrained smile that had been on my face since I met them.

"Oh my, that's wonderful, Darius! It was your destiny to find them here." Nisrina said with a beaming smile. Her eyes glistened with tears of happiness for me. She had felt like another mother figure to me, and I was over the moon that she was happy for me.

"I am happy for you too," Sofia added.

I didn't notice that Hamid had entered the room until he was about to take his seat. "What happened?" He looked at Nisrina. "You all are happy about something, and I must know. I've had a stressful day. Maybe whatever you all are smiling at will improve my day."

"Darius found his parents. They came by today to pick up their grain and wheat." Nisrina said.

"Oh, that is amazing," his eyes were as wide as an owl's.

There was a moment of silence.

"—Darius?" Noah tried getting my attention.

"Um, yes?" I asked him with the same smile on my face.

"I asked if you would see them tomorrow."

"Oh yes! I might leave before we eat breakfast. There's so much I have to ask them."

Hamid placed his cup on the table after drinking water. "Nonsense. When you wake up, come down here and ask for breakfast; someone will serve you. There's always someone down here, starting at four in the morning."

I nodded.

"Also, if you go before we wake up, I will have an official take you. He will take you to where they live and wait for you to bring you back."

I wondered how they had their address, and then I remembered they took down everyone's address when they picked up grain and wheat. "Okay, thank you."

There was another moment of silence, and the servers came out with dinner. It smelt amazing—or maybe it was just my jubilant mood.

"So, does this mean you no longer need to leave?" Hamid asked me as he took his first bite of a sandwich, maintaining eye contact.

"Not anymore. I couldn't be any happier now, mostly." I told him. I had one favor to ask of him. I knew it would be beyond the bounds of what was possible, but the worst that could happen was he would laugh at me and tell me no. I didn't plan on telling him until the last day I worked in the palace.

Later that night, I lay in bed trying to get some sleep, but it was impossible. And how had I ended up in Morocco, when we were from Egypt? I didn't end up falling asleep until late at night—the last time I checked the time it was one in the morning.

I had my alarm set for six in the morning, as usual. I quickly got ready and rushed down to the dining room, where I ate breakfast rapidly. An official was waiting for me; Hamid must have told him of my plans.

"Just let me know when you want to go, and I will take you there. I already looked up where they lived." The official said.

I gobbled down the remaining food and eagerly got up from my seat. The official led me to a car parked in front of the palace, and we drove there in silence. The weather matched my mood— it was sunny without a cloud in the sky.

"They live on the first floor of this building," the official told me when we arrived. "I will wait for you here."

The neighborhood looked sketchy, and no one was walking around outside. All the buildings had three or more levels, and every one of them was worn down with peeling paint. The door of my parents' building was wide open, and I entered cautiously. Ahead of me was a set of stairs, and to my left was a door—that must be them. I knocked on the door, and within seconds the door flew open.

"Darius, my dear boy!" My mother rushed towards me and hugged me tightly. "Please come in."

I walked into their apartment. It was smaller than my home back in Morocco, and the restroom was right beside the door. The kitchen was across from the bathroom, which was as small as my bedroom back in Morocco. She walked in front of me, and I followed her. There was a room near the bathroom, about twice the size of the kitchen. At the end of the narrow hallway was another room of the same size that they used as a living room.

My dad was lying down on a sidari. As soon as he saw me, he got up and hugged me tightly.

We sat down, and my dad spoke first. "Would you like to start, or should we?"

"I think you should. Can you start from the beginning, with how I got abducted?"

"I was sitting down with Karim at a park while you were playing on the swing," my mom began. "You used to make new friends so easily when you were young. You would always talk to everyone at the park. A hooded man ran — my mom broke into tears before she could finish, and we lapsed into silence for a moment. There was a part of me that felt guilty for getting abducted—like if I hadn't been so outgoing, maybe it wouldn't have been so easy for someone to take me.

My dad picked up where my mom left off. "The man picked you up and ran away. He got into a car, and that was the last time we saw him. I tried chasing after you, but he had been close to the car and I wasn't fast enough."

"Did you report it to the police?"

"Plenty of times, but they couldn't find you anywhere." My dad said, and my mom left the living room. "They must have sent you to Morocco right after they took you away from us."

There was another quiet moment. I looked at my father's blank stare. Out of all the children, they chose me. Maybe it was random, but they must have planned it out cautiously if they factored in sending me to a different country.

My mom came back carrying a metal platter that had three cups and a beaker of some blended juice.

"What happened on your end?" My dad asked as my mom handed me a cup of juice. I took the first sip and was pleased to taste freshly squeezed orange juice.

"Two people who are much older than you adopted me. Their names are Ahmed and Fatima," I said.

"Ahmed and Fatima?" My dad's eyebrows knitted together. "Hmm."

"Yes. Ever since I was young, I've helped Ahmed at his shop in the market. Throughout the years, I learned the craft of selling and dealing with people, and I made a lot of friends there."

"Did they have any children of their own?" My mom asked.

"No, they didn't… that's why they adopted me. But I never knew the real reason I was in the orphanage."

"They didn't tell you? Or did you not bother to ask?" my dad asked me suspiciously.

"Well, the orphanage knew nothing more than my name, not even who left me there," I told them.

My parents looked at each other.

"A couple of months ago, I had a dream of us somewhere in Egypt, with the pyramids and your hands tied. I could barely remember your faces, which is why it took me some time yesterday to recognize you both."

My mom smiled and looked at my dad as he said, "You've grown up so much. From six years old to twenty." I nodded with a gentle smile on my face.

"In your dream, was it only us, or was there someone else?" My mom asked me.

"It was only the three of us, but the last one was different. There was someone else holding two little kids."

"You were born here and raised here until we got separated," my dad said. "Those dreams made you travel out here?"

"Yes—after I started having them more frequently, I told Ahmed and Fatima that I had to find out for myself. At first, they didn't want me to go because it was dangerous, but I couldn't give up the chance of finding you two."

"I have a bad feeling about this person. Why would he not support you?" My dad said. "If I were in his place, I would support the person I was taking care of fully. I would understand why he wouldn't if you were young, but you're a man now."

My mom looked at him reproachfully. "He probably didn't want him to get lost or hurt and lose another family."

My mom had a point. I'd never thought about it that way. They might have wanted me to stay so I wouldn't get disappointed. Their reasons were all borne out of their love and care for me—as was their decision to let me go. They knew I would regret it otherwise.

I continued to explain my journey to them until the moment I met them at the King's palace. They sat there, listening to all of it until the very end.

"So every difficulty you had helped you reach us?"

"Yes, now that I think about it."

There was a moment of silence.

"Time has flown by - I should get back to the palace. I only have a couple of days left until I finish my job."

My dad looked at the clock above their small television. "Time flies by." Books were surrounding the television. My parents, too, must have loved to read. I didn't know what type of books they had.

"There is one thing I would like to tell you, though," I said and waited for them to respond. I didn't know if it was the right time to tell them or to wait.

"Yes? What is it?"

"I made a deal with the king. If I helped him out, he would help me find you. Since I have already found you two, I no longer need to find you again." I laughed. And then, with a serious expression, I added: "I want to marry the king's daughter."

My dad suppressed a laugh, while my mom's face was blank.

"Are you serious?" My dad asked me. He was trying his best to cover his laughter—mostly unsuccessfully.

"Yes. It doesn't hurt to try, right?" I would ask him on my last day. "What's the worst that can happen?"

"You can try, but I don't think he will approve. If you think she has good morals and character, then I support you. I am sure Amina supports you too." He said. "Look at where we live, Darius. No king would want his daughter to marry someone that comes from a family like ours."

I understood what he meant. The king would most likely prefer his daughter to marry someone with a rich household, or even another prince. I liked to think I had good qualities, but I didn't know if they were worth anything to the king.

"Unless the king has other plans, it's practically impossible - but you can try. As you said, he won't imprison you for asking. Since you work there, it's better you than a random person walking through the front door!"

My parents were on board with the idea, and now all I required was the approval of the King and Queen—that would be the hard part.

"You said this person's name is Ahmed?" My Dad asked.

"Yes… Dad, it's nothing. He's a good man; I'm sure he had nothing to do with my abduction."

He said nothing else, so I said goodbye to both of them. I promised them I would return every morning to be with them.

The official started the car, and I got in. The neighborhood was more crowded than when I'd arrived, and it made me wonder. We drove back in silence, and I was glad of it. All the officials looked as if someone had sucked all the happiness out of their bodies, except for Noah. He was the only official I knew who smiled more than he frowned. The ride back was longer than I remembered—but then again, I had been more preoccupied and excited that morning.

The following week flew by. I spent my mornings at my parents' home and the afternoons working at the palace. I also planned how and when to ask the king for Sofia's hand. I decided that after dinner on my last day was the best time. Hamid was always in a good mood after dinner.

I hadn't seen Sofia much of late, as I visited my parents in the mornings rather than attend lessons with her. But her approval was as important as Hamid's—there was no point in trying to marry her if she wasn't interested.

Before dinnertime, I started packing my things. There wasn't much, but the king had given me some clothes and some gifts throughout the time I had stayed in the palace. He had been gracious to me, almost as if I were his son.

I was the last one to sit down at the dinner table.

"How are your parents?" Nisrina asked me.

"They're good. My dad has been a little tired as of late, but he's feeling better." I told her. He worked at a shop, and the owner had been treating him unfairly, making him work long hours for little pay.

We mostly ate dinner in silence.

I looked at Sofia. She probably didn't like small talk either, which would explain why she didn't speak much. It was difficult for me to be sure.

"Hamid, could I talk to you in private after dinner?" I asked him bluntly, breaking the silence that had fallen over the table. I was eager to know what the other favor he wanted to ask of me was, but I wasn't sure if I should ask about that or Sofia first. He looked at Nisrina, who was sitting beside him, and swallowed the food in his mouth before speaking.

"Sure thing."

After he finished eating, we went out into the hallway. No one was around.

"What do you want to ask me?"

"Well, I want to ask you something, but I also want to know why you chose me to do this job."

He looked down the hall and then back at me. "I was planning to tell you tomorrow when you were about to leave. But as it's just the two of us, I will tell you now—but only after you have asked your question."

I took a deep breath and rubbed my hands together. My palms had grown sweaty, and my heart was racing. I felt almost as if I were about to faint. But it was now or never. I reminded myself that the worst thing he could do was laugh at me.

"I wanted to ask you and put it out there. So please—"

"Spit it out, ask me. Don't be shy."

"I would like to marry your daughter."

My legs felt like pudding, and I used the wall behind me to prop myself up as Hamid broke into laughter, slapping his thighs. This was it; he would tell me no and make me collect my things and leave.

"Are you ready to hear what I have to ask of you?" he said after he settled down and stopped laughing. I wasn't ready; he had laughed at me and didn't even respond to my question. But he was the king, and I couldn't ignore him.

"Could you please answer me first?"

He ignored me and went on, "So the reason I wanted you to work here was to… are you ready for this?" He stopped, and I continued laughing.

"No," I whispered under my breath.

"I wanted you to marry my daughter."

I froze. Everything went silent; I couldn't hear anything and everything was foggy. My heart wanted to pound right out of my chest, and I went numb all over. His words kept blaring in my head, flashing in neon red.

"Are you well?" Hamid shook me by the shoulders.

I coughed to clear my throat, giving me a chance to find my voice again. "Are... you... serious?"

"Yes, but there is something you need to know before I hand her to you." He said, no longer smiling, and sounding a lot more serious.

"What is it? Does she even want to marry me?"

"Well, since Nisrina and I can't have children anymore, I would like my grandchildren to have my last name instead of yours. No offense."

It was a difficult decision to make. I was the only child my parents had, so my family name would end with me. The only way for my family name to continue was if my dad had any brothers. He had never spoken of any.

"I don't know. I will need to ask my parents first."

"Sofia and Nisrina have already agreed, so we'll only need your family's approval," he told me.

I finally relaxed, and I could think once more. "But why me? Why not someone else?"

"Good question. I wanted you because I felt like I already knew you more than any stranger I could pick. Noah spoke highly of you, and I thought you possessed good qualities."

"You know that I am not rich and my family lives in a small home?" I asked him.

"Exactly. That's another reason we wanted you. I didn't want Sofia to marry someone who was rich, and she didn't want a rich person either. I want my daughter to marry someone who has good qualities. Besides, we already have enough money. She wants to marry you, so it has worked out for all of us as long as your parents approve."

"Let's go back inside. Noah is waiting for me to review the amounts of wheat and grain we gave out this month." I followed him back inside. "I won't tell anyone about this until you tell me what your parents think. Let me know by tomorrow. I will have an official drive you home as usual. Come back for lunch and tell me. You can bring your parents as well if you'd like."

"Everything all right?" Noah asked when we had entered.

"Yeah, we're good. Darius, you can go up to bed or stay with us, whatever you'd like." Hamid told me.

"I'm a little tired. I think I'll rest up. Goodnight," I said, and headed out the door that led to the staircase.

The next morning, I went to my parents' to tell them about the good news. There were some days when I only found my mom at home as my dad had to work, but today they were both at home.

"I have some news I have to tell you," I told my mom as she greeted me.

"Good or bad?" My mom asked me to follow her back to the living room. "Isn't today your last day at the palace?"

"Good news, and yes, today is my last day."

I greeted my father, who was lying down and watching television. I waited until I had both of their attention, and I spilled out the news.

"So, the king asked you to marry his daughter, but your children must take his daughter's last name?" My dad asked.

"Yes," I looked up.

"Do it, son, forget about the last name! If you marry her, you won't have to worry about money. You will live freely. Do you want to marry her?" My dad asked.

"Yes, Dad, I told you last time."

"Did the king tell his daughter and wife about this? Do they approve?" My mom asked.

"The whole family approves. We only need the two of you to

give your approval."

"You have it." My mom smiled.

At lunch that day, I told Hamid the great news in front of everyone, as it was no longer important to hide it. Noah was the first to congratulate me as I sat next to him.

"We'll set up a big wedding for you two. Would your parents be able to come to the palace tonight to talk more in depth about the wedding?" Hamid asked me.

"Yes, they can," I told him, pleased as anything.

For the next week, my family and Sofia's family set up everything for the wedding, and not long after that, we got married.

Later that night, the Kind and Queen welcomed my parents to the palace for dinner. They spoke to the King and Queen about the marriage between Sofia and me. As the bridegroom, they expected my family to pay a certain amount of money to Sofia's family. Not that the King needed any more money than he already had. It was more for the culture.

We set up a date for the following summer. The King would cover all the costs of the wedding. I didn't have much family to bring to the wedding unless there was a way to transport all my friends from Morocco to Egypt for the summer. I was sure the King would find a way.

The King and Queen invited my parents and me to stay overnight, as we stayed up past midnight talking about the wedding.

As we were heading upstairs, someone crossed my mind. Adam. I never asked Hamid what his punishment was. I called Hamid as I was walking one or two meters behind them. Hamid slowed down until I caught up. My parents, along with Nisrina, kept walking in front of us. Nisrina and my mom were talking about something, but I couldn't catch what it was.

"Can you tell me what you did to Adam? How long is he staying in jail?" I asked.

"Not long. I will put him in for fifteen years. He stole and lied." Hamid said. He rested his arm on my shoulders and brought me closer to his side. I looked at him as he was tugging his beard. His eyes focused in front of us. "You made me rethink his sentence. I was so inspired by how you forgave him. You two were friends, correct?"

"Yes. I knew him in Morocco. He told me about traveling across the desert. He had it tough growing up. That doesn't give him the right to steal or lie. We all had it tough somehow."

"Well, I lowered his sentence to only a year. He's scheduled for release next year. I will keep a close watch on him if he stays in Egypt."

"Okay. That was nice of you to lower his sentence." I said.

We approached my room in the palace. "Darius, you already know your room," Nisrina said. "Amina and Karim, you can sleep in this room." She pointed to a room across from mine. "Everything you'll need should be in there. If you need anything and you can't find it, come ask me. Our room in down the hall to the right." Nisrina smiled and lightly tapped Amina's shoulder.

"Sounds great. Thank you." My mom said.

Hamid and Nisrina continued down the hall to their bedroom. Just before I wanted to say goodnight to my parents, my dad placed his arm on my shoulder. Slightly pushed me into the room. He didn't say a word. I felt my mom walking behind us. My mom closed the door to my room, and then I asked my dad, "Is there something you'd like to tell me?" I turned towards him. His eyes were wide open. He was looking behind me. He said nothing. My room was so silent that I heard Hamid and Nisrina's door close from down the hall.

I jumped up on my bed, and both my parents sat at the edge of my bed. They both twisted toward me. My dad said, "Do you have a picture of Ahmed?"

His face was serious, and I didn't know why it mattered if I had a picture or not. I would visit him soon, and my parents could accompany me. "Why do you want to see a picture of him?" I had a picture of him. Ahmed gave me a picture of him and Fatima before I left.

"Do you have a picture or not?" I haven't seen my dad this serious. He was determined to see a picture. I obeyed my father's wish. I got up off my bed and looked inside my bag for the picture of Ahmed and Fatima. After a couple of moments, I pulled it out and looked at it for a few seconds. Memories ran through my head from the market to waking up early in the morning to the ticking sound in the kitchen.

I turned around towards my parents and handed the picture to my dad. I sat back on my bed with my legs crossed, patiently waiting to hear what he would say. They focused on the picture as I inspected their facial expressions. Amina pulled back and said, "They seem like good people."

I smiled as I made eye contact with my mom. "They are."

"I know this man." My dad said as he handed me the picture. He sounded very confident and firm.

"What?" I looked back down at the picture of Ahmed and Fatima. Intrigued by what my father said. Ahmed lived thousands of miles away; surely my dad made a mistake.

By the time I picked up my head, they were standing by the door. "Dad, how do you know him?" I asked. My dad looked at me and then back at Amina.

He looked back at me again, "Ahmed is my cousin."

I didn't know what to think. My mouth was wide open. It didn't make any sense at first. After I recollected my thoughts, I said, "Are you positive?"

"What's his last name?" My dad asked quickly.

"It's Majid," I said.

"I am one hundred percent sure. He looks the same from when he was a kid. He also has the same last name. My father and his mother are siblings." My dad said. "I'm a little tired son."

"Goodnight," my parents said. They opened the door to my room and turned the lights off before they left.

"Goodnight" I replied. I laid flat on my bed. Looking at the ceiling of the room. Small lights from outside crept inside the room between the long curtains. I rested my head on the fluffy pillow. Thoughts bounced in my head. My dad and Ahmed are cousins. All these years I lived with my dad's cousin.

Zak Attioui graduated from the University of Massachusetts Lowell with a degree in Civil Engineering and English. He currently lives in Boston, Massachusetts. When he's not writing, he loves to travel, study different subjects, or play videos games. You can find more of his writing at www.attiouiwrites.com

www.ingramcontent.com/pod-product-compliance
Lightning Source LLC
Chambersburg PA
CBHW051440130726
47987CB00005B/2133